The Arrangement

By Yvonne Sibanda

1

Chapter 1

Harmony, 2009

One glance at him, is all it took for Margaret Fletcher to dislike him instantly. Whatever confidence she had, plummeted down to her heeled toes, as her supposedly blind date turned out to be everything that she did not want.

Perfect.

Garret Henderson took off the dark tinted glasses, then looked around him before his eyes zeroed in on her. For a brief moment, Margaret felt like she was impaled to the wall, by the intense gaze that stripped her of every sense of pretense she'd put up.

Gulping down a few quick breaths, her modest dress proving to not be that under his unwavering gaze, Margaret wiped her sweaty palms on the side.

Oh brother, this is a mess, she thought in a daze. Cathy, her best friend, hadn't been lying after all when she mentioned the handsome face and broad physique, in fact she had downplayed it.

In no way would Margaret be able to convince her sweet mother that Garret Henderson wasn't suitable.

She'd been kidding herself all the way, while she drove to the restaurant, thinking she would meet a young man, who would watch her with horror filled eyes and flee without looking back, the instant she played out the drama she'd instore for him.

This man coming to meet her was probably made of sterner stuff and wouldn't bat an eyelid.

What if he settled for her?

Did this mean that she was to become like her mother, never herself but striving to be perfect in all ways, so she remained relevant to the man in her life?

Who ever heard of a handsome man being faithful to one woman?

Well, she hadn't.

Why was she even considering him in those terms?

A while ago Margaret Fletcher was averse to the thought of getting married!

This meeting was merely a formality on her part, something that could be considered, *'the reasonable thing to do,'* when a parent asked.

Gulping down a few breaths, she looked for a way of escape, knowing she was between a rock and a hard place.

This is definitely not going to work; frantically she thought and briefly shut her eyes, in the hopes that the man would disappear and this would turn out to have been one of those nightmares, that one woke up from in a panic, until it dawned that it had all been a dream, then they moved on with their lives just like nothing had happened.

The piercing gaze could still be felt on her skin and she slowly opened her eyes, dismay in the slouch of her shoulders and pouted lips as the man kept on walking towards her.

For a brief second, Margaret could have given everything for the man coming her way not to be Garret Henderson but one who had mixed-up his dates.

Why by the way, was she the one meant to elevate her mother's status in her life?

She didn't ask to be brought into this world so she could pander to her parent's wishes. Forget about her mother's furiously flung words at the family gathering. She just wasn't her, no matter how her mother tried to turn her into a miniaturized version of herself.

The fact that Margaret had survived high school without having a boyfriend, or falling pregnant, should be proof enough that they were not cut from the same cloth.

Watching in apprehension, as Garret sauntered to her, with that self-assured air clinging to him like a second skin, Margaret deeply exhaled and resigned herself to smiling, in fact clenching her teeth through the process, with the thought of escaping as soon as an opportunity presented itself.

"Hi, are you Margaret Fletcher, I'm Garret Henderson," Garret introduced in a deep voice, more on the husky side like a person who smoked and stretched out his hand to her. *Really even his voice had to be sexy.*

She nearly answered, "I am sorry sir, you've made a mistake, I'm Catherine Gooding," then walked out of that restaurant like her pants were on fire. But she wasn't that cruel and found herself instead replying in a soft voice, "Yes—uhm hi, nice to meet you Garret."

Even though slightly shaky, at least it was a great improvement from the strident panicked one in her mind. Margaret shook his hand and settled back on the chair.

Why did he have to be so damn handsome?

Why, she almost yelled.

For that reason, she was now having second thoughts and about to cringe in mortification over the way she'd dressed.

Her mother had definitely outdone herself this time, even though fully aware that handsome men were not what her daughter was comfortable around.

How could she be, after she'd witnessed her father's vanity, and on how her mother tried to keep up with him?

All that endless devotion to him and his smooth, seductive being, that managed to make her stay like the two women before her. What did her father then do to her mother? He was quick to relegate her to the title of third wife and not last like he had promised her, once she lost flavor in his sight. By flavor meaning *marriage*. Whenever Fletcher married his women, he appeared to lose interest quicker than the mental span of a toddler.

The first and second wives laughed at Beulah's expense after witnessing her downfall. For a few years Beulah thought that she was different from them by far and they were more than happy, when her assumption was proved wrong.

"Shall we order?" Garret asked her and Marg nodded before they placed their order to the waiter.

After the food was delivered to their table, she toyed with it, at a loss of what to say. The food at Honeys melted on the palette like butter and every texture and flavor could be tasted within. Currently though, she didn't feel like putting a morsel into her mouth.

Garret wasn't speaking, which was rather a huge deal to her. Men who loved to talk often gave her clues on their psyche, hence from that, her reason for running away from the date could be established.

With her mind, she urged him to talk and dismiss her. The silence stretched on unabated, while a few muted voices from the other clients in the restaurant floated to them.

Marg, seeing no way out of this, placed the fork and knife into the plate and softly spoke. "Look, it's been nice meeting you. Our families are well meaning but I don't think we will work. Just inform your parents that I'm not the right girl for you," she finished with bated breath and watched Garret take his time, as he painstakingly and with deliberate ease, took the napkin on the side, then wiped his hands.

Garret finally raised a brow at the lady seated across from him. Interesting indeed, he mused. Margaret Fletcher was literally perched at the edge of the chair and about to bolt. This was the first time when a woman had reacted in this manner when meeting him and for some reason, he was enjoying seeing her squirm.

Bravo pastor Garret, It's official, you're now a nutcase.

How couldn't he be, after the endless dates his mom was subjecting him to, which always ended with him making a fast trot to the door. He'd discovered the notion that women were the gentle and fairer sex, questionable, as the ones he had met so far turned to be aggressive beings, who would do whatever it took to get the coveted title of being called Mrs. Henderson.

His guard had gone up too at seeing Margaret for the first time. He realized why his mother must have recommended Margaret. From her outer appearance, she would definitely make the perfect Pastor's wife without breaking a sweat.

Out of curiosity he asked her, "Why do you think this will not work?"

Another first-time experience, the women he'd met before had plenty of reasons on why it would work.

Margaret's eyes widened at his question.

"I was given the impression that I'll be meeting a junior pastor not this."

Garret corked his brow and crossed his arms over his broad chest. "What do you mean not this? I'm a junior pastor after all."

Was Margaret one of those who figured a junior pastor was meant to look humble—implying impoverished. Garret studied her every movement as he waited on her reply, while she continued to chew her bottom lip.

"It's just that—," her speech faltered and she cringed when he narrowed his eyes on her.

"I get it," Garret cut off her lame attempt with the dismissive wave of his hand. "You'd assumed that you will meet a shabbily dressed man who's not in touch with the world. Am I to understand that I'm being judged by the way I look?"

"No, it's not that."

"What is it then Margaret?"

Margaret inhaled sharply over the unforgiving tone.

Was he angry with her?

She looked at him. Yep, the man seated across from her was definitely irritated and things were getting much trickier than she could have anticipated.

He was correct on one fact too; she definitely had judged him. The assessing, irritated eyes, confirmed her first thoughts. A mere mortal like her would not survive if he decided to put on his charm. She was her mother's daughter after all.

"Garret, it's not about you but it's about me. I want a man who will be faithful and loyal to the vows that he makes."

"And you think I will not be like that?" He stared at her in disbelief while she bit her tongue. There she'd gone again, digging her own grave without thinking she would fail to come out of it once she jumped.

"You can have any girl you want," she desperately said and Garret nearly laughed at her anxious expression.

Isn't this what he wanted too?

Margaret was giving him a great opportunity after all. Thirteen girls in counting had tried to paw at him and get married to him, while he proved his dear mother on how wrong they were for him, and here was one who wasn't throwing a fuss but rather wanted to cut the date short.

He should be relieved right, that this tiny woman with the cute orange glossed lips, didn't want anything to do with him, especially with the prospect of being tied to his rich, influential family, which appeared to not appeal to her at all.

"Hmmm," he scratched his chin. Why then did he not feel like letting Margaret go? Maybe this was all an act. She might have heard from the other women on how hard they'd tried and decided to act the opposite.

He watched her bite her lower lip and take the fork before she toyed with her food again.

What had his mother said? She was Fletcher's daughter from his third marriage. Everyone of course knew about Fletcher because of his musically talented sons, who were making hits in the music industry. An interview had been done pertaining to the twins' lives and family. In counting, their father now had five wives.

Wait a minute, had Marg pegged him as a player. A loyal, faithful husband is what she needed, he grimaced at the recollection.

Making up his mind, Garret carefully chose his words, assessing her with his brooding eyes and said, "one month," then watched her snap her head up while her eyes widened.

Her reaction gave her away. She wasn't acting. She really wanted to get out of the situation. She was perfect. A shadow of a smile flitted through on his lips.

Marg frowned and asked, "One month of what?"

"You can call this our little arrangement. Date me for a month." Pretend you are dating me, but he wasn't going to say that out loud, not yet.

"Why would you suggest that? As you must be aware by now, I don't like you."

Garret laughed. "That Marg is the reason why I think you are perfect. Just one month in which I'll prove to you how wrong you are about me and the fact that I'm not like any man you know."

Marg scoffed at that declaration. He really was full of himself as she'd thought. "Why would you want to change my opinion on that? What's in it for you?"

A crooked smile appeared on his handsome face before he answered, "Maybe, my getting to know you better, might prove me wrong over my first impression of you."

"What do you mean?" A frown creased her delicate brows.

He dismissively shrugged his shoulders and replied. "In that you are a snob."

Her mouth dropped open in shock.

Chapter 2

"My little munchkin you are back," Beulah excitedly said before she got into Margaret's room and hugged her. A gust of the flowery perfume her mother usually wore entered along with her.

"How was your date with Garret Henderson?"

A disaster, Marg thought of saying but kept quiet and resumed with her book instead. Her mom as usual was dressed in one of those skimpy outfits that said, baby let's have a little bit of fun. Marg frowned at the get up; this meant her dad would be coming over.

"Your aunt said you will get along well. My darling girl is to be the pastor's wife and will be tied to the most influential family of all. I can't wait to see Dorothy and the rest of the women die of envy."

Great, just great. Her mother was only doing this so she'd one point above the rest of the co-wives.

Margaret was still smarting from Garret having called her a snob. Of all things, how could he say that? Was her mother sure about him being a pastor?

Speculatively looking at her, she asked her, "Mom, is Garret truly a pastor?"

"What a silly question to ask. You would have known all these things if you removed your head from your books for a second." Her mother narrowed her eyes at the book in her hand while Marg sat cross legged on the bed.

"Your aunt assured me that he's a good man, above reproach if that's what you are worried about. Don't you attend the same church?"

Typical of her mother who had never stepped foot in a church, she thought all of them were the same. Her barb over her not paying attention to anything else still managed to hit home despite her having heard it a countless number of times. What was wrong with her in trying to break from the norm?

"No, I don't attend his church ma."

"He's perfect for you right?" Her mother pleadingly looked at her. "It's a step up from the other young men. You did mention the only reason they were not good enough is because they didn't uphold the same values like you."

Audibly sighing, Marg contemplated on how reasoning with her mom was pointless. All she thought of were things that pertained to catering to the needs of the flesh, when she'd in fact added in her argument that the reason why she didn't want to settle down was because she needed her independence before she thought of marriage. As usual, she must not have heard her.

"Can you think of anything else rather than getting your only daughter married as proof that you raised her right?"

"Like what?"

"I told you I want to go to varsity, and study psychology. My friends are at varsity ma. Living their lives as independent women, while I'm stuck here in this old huge mansion, filled with step moms and half-brothers who think I'm not allowed to have a functional brain."

Her mom flagged her arms dismissively. "Don't be silly darling. Getting married is a noble thing. High school education is enough. What is this talk about independence, it's overrated Marg. Ask your friends a few years down the line and you will come to realize that you will be in a much better position for having settled down; while in their quest to be 'independent' they lost much more. Better yet, if you feel like you still want to go to university after making those babies, your husband will send you there."

That was it, the crux of the matter, Marg thought as she looked helplessly at the woman who gave birth to her.

Her mother was one of the women who had been brainwashed into thinking their main purpose in life was to cater for a man's needs. She knew her mom had the money to send her off to varsity but because of her archaic beliefs she wasn't willing to help her out.

They had passed the dark era, but with women who still thought like her mother, she definitely knew that men would always justify their actions on never being faithful to one woman. If a woman was independent and didn't have to act like a man was a god, then the bloody men were bound to realize that they could be dispensable too.

Her alarm clock rang and she reached out to it, on the side of the bed before promptly switching it off. Standing up to straighten her bed, Marg was quick to say, "Time for me to get ready for work, and time for you to get rid of those, we wouldn't want to disappoint our dear husband, would we," adopting her mom's seductive purr while she pointed at the rollers still in her hair.

"Margaret Fletcher, you haven't yet told me how your date went," her mom sulked. She surely could be a whiner at times while Marg was relegated to acting like an adult.

Marg rolled her eyes. At no point at all would she inform her mom that the date was a total disaster, especially the last part where she acted impulsively as she was prone to.

Her mom shrugged her shoulders dismissively. "I still don't think it's necessary for you to be doing this waitressing job. Once your father hears about it, he's bound to put an end to it. If you were to be with Garret, all these problems would disappear just like that."

"News flash ma, I and Garret aren't an item." And we might never be. "So don't count those chicks before they've hatched."

Her mom snorted and mumbled over having a rebellious daughter while Marg huffed and rushed to take a shower before she left for work.

Marg scowled at the couple seated at the table in the middle of the hotel restaurant. She knew she was being unreasonable with the way she was acting but still, couldn't stop her laser eyes from fleecing the man into mincemeat.

There was never a day she had come face to face with his royal highness, Garret Henderson. After having met him on the ill-fated date, apparently fate had decided that they meet again, at her workplace this time around. Lucky her.

She had been right after all with the assumption of him being a player, seeing he was now with another girl, having forgotten about the little arrangement he'd proposed on their date, before her outburst, that is.

Her presence appeared not to bother him in the least and at the fact that she had caught him doing exactly what he had denied before, entertaining floozies. Instead of running for cover because of an all-consuming shame, Garret merely raised a brow at her and continued charming the gills off his date.

Ok, so he did posh with floozies, while he took out decent girls like her to Honeys.

She knew her thoughts were uncalled for since Simone Richards wasn't a floozy, but happened to be one of those entitled, rich, spoilt brats who thought everything revolved around them.

Simone giggled at something Garret said to her and grasped his hand while he covered it with his. Marg wordlessly opened her mouth in shock. Pastor my foot, she bitterly thought still watching the couple, before the sound of a bell had her turning aside to grab the order that was now ready.

Quick strides to the table are all it took so she got the hell out of there, before she did something she would later regret, like literally puke at the couple, since their lovey dovey had made her throw up in her mouth already.

Placing the tray and taking out the dishes, she pasted a stiff smile and took a step away from them.

"Miss, sorry, I appear to have dropped my fork, please be a dear and get me another one." Garret called out to her. Marg balled her hands into fists, turned around to face him before she smiled. Oh, how that smile pained her. "There's no need to apologize, it's no bother since I am here to serve you." She strode to the table drawer where they kept their clean cutlery before she went back to Garrets' table.

"There you go sir," she whispered.

"Eh, miss, the water is not cold enough…" then from then onwards she was in the hands of a pastor from hell since his demands became more and more ridiculous. From the barely hot soup, the warm water, the falling cutlery, like he just enjoyed keeping her on her toes. Finally, she snapped.

Stumbling on the tiled floor, she watched in fascination as the bucket of ice-cold water flew to his lap, spilling some of it onto the front of his tailor-made suit.

"I am so sorry," she wailed in horror at her blunder while she could evidently see the irritation set in Garret's eyes before he attempted to shake off the cold drench, after having abruptly stood up from the chair in shock. He excused himself and walked to the restroom.

A ghost of a smile appeared on her face. The strutting rooster had just tasted his own medicine.

"You did that on purpose," Simone commented.

"Sorry." Marg adopted a bland smile.

"I mean you did that on purpose, I saw it."

"I don't know what you are talking about."

"The water thingy. In no way would you have possibly tripped from there." Simone looked at the flat tiled floor skeptically. Marg huffed. "You got it all wrong. Please excuse me; I need to attend to the other clients."

While they were talking, Yolanda, another waitress who happened to be on duty with Marg, swiftly and efficiently mopped the floor then walked away. Marg was about to walk after her and thank her when Simone grabbed her sleeve, halting her retreat.

"Hey," she yelled. Ralph the head waiter swiftly walked up to where she was.

"Ma'am, is there something wrong?" He asked Simone while he frowned at Marg.

"Your staff is rude and should be severely punished," she said with a pout on her lips.

"Do you mind explaining to me what happened? Margaret is one of our best employees and the epitome of good behavior."

"I don't know about that but what she did was uncalled for," Simone sneered. She went on to explain to the waiter what happened. Marg was relieved that only a few customers were in the restaurant, intent on eating their meal, rather than watch the drama unfolding in their midst.

She felt like skinning the tramp for not letting things go. Simone was such an attention seeker and to think they had been in the same class at high school. She was never a fan of Simone and till to date, she still wasn't.

Simone was now at Fashion College and making something of herself, while she had to die of envy over her good fortune. Not that she was envious of Simone, her mind scoffed at the thought. Her main concern was if she ever was going to get over the Fletcher curse and be independent like her.

"Your waitress," Simone ground out and had Marg imagining a school headmistress, using their sharp, long nails to scratch on the surface of the blackboard. "Needs to apologize to Garret."

Garret was just coming out from drying his suit. Marg had made him numb on his manhood with that ice cold water stance. Just like he appeared to rub her the wrong way, she did the same to him.

He couldn't believe it when he got into the hotel restaurant and caught sight of her, prettily smiling to one of the patrons and taking up their order before she walked to his table.

For a second he thought that maybe he was looking at her twin, until she balefully looked at him like he had committed the worst crime by going on a date with Simone.

He couldn't keep his eyes off her, that slow pull he had felt suddenly tugging at his sleeve again. What was it with her that made him feel like he was on a see-saw instead of steady, solid ground?

Simone stroked his hand, having asked something of him which apparently had fallen on his deaf ears since his whole focus was on Marg.

Garret found himself clearing his throat and trying to concentrate on his date. The little beauty laughed at something one of the patrons whispered to her after calling her aside before she winked and glided from him. Garret pulled at his tie suddenly feeling hot. Her hips slightly swayed. She was an eye catcher considering the males who were there were looking at her in the same manner he was.

For some insane reason he thought it would be fun to goad her into revealing a temper he knew lurked beyond the calm demeanor. The temper that had flared on him, when he had announced that she was a snob and the same temper that was now surely building up, evidenced by the dagger piercing eyes slowly fleecing his skin, as she waited for their order. Any sensible man could have run for cover, but he has never been sensible and wasn't going to start now.

"Garret!" Simone snapped, before she smiled at his raised brow at her tone. "Darling, I was thinking, next time we meet somewhere else other than here." She placed her hand over his, while he regretfully reached to it, so he removed it without hurting her feelings.

In no way would he meet her for a second date. She just wasn't his type.

He groaned and pinched the bridge of his nose seeing he had been right about Simone. She was an attention seeker.

"Apologize," Simone was curtly saying as Garret walked up to them after having dried his suit in the restroom. Marg crossed her arms over her breasts and furiously glared at her.

"You see, a severe punishment is what she needs or else Mr. Henderson will no longer be your client from now on."

Ralph inhaled sharply while a flicker akin to fear passed Marg's eyes as she quickly dropped her arms and looked to Garret who had joined them.

For goodness' sake, she was just starting to earn her way to freedom; did Simone have to be so heartless?

"Easy," Garret intruded. "There's no need for her to apologize."

"Why not?" Simone asked. "Don't tell me darling that you feel pity for the silly girl."

Garret saw the glare; Marg was likely to do something she would later regret. For some reason he knew the little lady wouldn't take being called silly lying down, she would surely lash back. This called for a time up. With Simone presuming her rights over him, that also signaled the end of their date. So, he sighed and adopted a bored expression on his date and slowly explained, "Because Simone, Marg has a right to be angry with me. Remember I have been trying to explain to you that I already have a woman in my life. Marg is her."

Simone and Ralph gasped at his announcement while Marg's eyes widened to saucers and her mouth had a comical 'o' shape.

Grabbing her hand quickly, he excused himself from Ralph and shocked Simone before literally dragging Marg out of there.

"What's up with you, why did you do that?" Marg yelled and managed to yank her hand from his.

"I am saving your job, is what I am doing, unless you do not have a need for it." Crossing his arms over his broad chest, Garret narrowed his eyes.

"Yaa right, by announcing to my supervisor and your floozy that I'm your woman."

"Simone is not my floozy," Garret growled, irritated at her assumption. Inhaling deeply, he calmed himself and softened his voice, "Do you know I happen to be a role model for the youths at my church. I don't have floozies as you put it."

"Good for you, I guess they haven't met the player in you, who asks for one month with one woman and on that same day takes another one out," Miss judgy pants retorted back.

Garret scoffed; this was getting out of hand. "Who hurt you?" He ground out. Marg flinched at the tone. "You know what Margaret; a simple question is always better than coming to a conclusion because you think you have a person figured out. Margaret Fletcher," his voice had turned hard this time, "the reason why I am with Simone is because my mom had already set up the date. You are not the only woman she had recommended to me."

If intimidation is what he intended, it wasn't going to work on her. She also glared at him, crossed her arms over her breasts and retorted. "Of course, right blame it on mommy dearest, she isn't here to defend herself after all." She pouted her cute lips and finished, "why didn't you refuse?"

oh wow, just wow, the little lady was messed up big time, Garret thought and leaned in to her, placing both his palms on the sides of the wall of the building. Marg leaned further away on the wall, her eyes suddenly becoming saucers and he could literally hear her sharp intake of breath.

"Marg," he growled. "Give me one good reason why I was meant to refuse my dear mom's wishes after the disastrous date I had with you?"

Marg squirmed from the penetrating gaze. Garret, up close and personal, was intimidating and she knew she had bitten more than she could swallow. And there was that other little thing he wasn't meant to find out.

"Hmm," he hummed and shifted from her, giving her the breather she desperately needed while she clutched at her tender heart. He softly spoke this time, having calmed down a bit, "Was I meant to refuse, the same way you refused when your mom asked you to meet with me."

Marg widened her eyes at him and flapped her hand dismissively. The man standing in front of her was merely pointing out that she was a hypocrite, she had also failed to refuse her mother's request. Her rattled senses were returning to her hence she flapped arms and retorted, "That is different."

"How so?"

"I didn't ask for a month to clear a preconceived notion."

Garret snorted before he replied, "fair enough. Mhm. You do have a point." Garret then grinned at her and added, "I did meet a couple of friends of yours afterwards."

Marg widened her eyes at him. Did she know how cute and innocent she looked when she did that? Not so brave after all, he thought.

"Speaking of chickening out where parents are concerned and saying no, I rather had an interesting conversation with, let me see," he flicked his fingers for emphasis, "two of your old friends. It was rather odd, you know, how they approached me after having spotted me with you. They were, mmmm—how do I phrase this? Rather vocal."

Marge clutched at her throat. Could Garret have figured it out? No, he wouldn't.

"Please do tell Marg, why would one guy claim you are an alcoholic, another a promiscuous woman, unless of course just like me, you failed to tell your parents and instead botched away the other blind dates like you did ours."

Marg slumped back her shoulders, cradled her face in her hands and wept.

Chapter 3

Garret watched in horror while Marg bawled her eyes out. The water works that always managed to get him somehow and leave him at a loss. She looked vulnerable and not at all the feisty girl he had witnessed ever since he met her.

How exciting, from having ladies throwing themselves at him, left, right and center—now he had suddenly turned into an ogre who made one cry. His small victory was turning out to be a flop. By the way, why was he being petty with Marg, like a girl with heightened emotions. Reaching out to her with a groan, he hugged her and whispered, "I am sorry," as he let her weep her frustrations out.

"Uhm, Marg you can take the rest of the day off, there are not a lot of clients today," Ralph advised once he got outside the hotel and found them in the hot embrace expected of lovers.

"Mr. Henderson, we called for a taxi for your lady friend."

Garret nodded and watched Ralph get back into the hotel.

Marg sniffled. Garret removed a clean hanky from his pocket and handed it to her.

"Show off," she whispered.

"Sorry—what?"

"You heard me. Show off. Mr. Henderson, we have called for a taxi for your lady friend."

Garret chuckled softly as Marg imitated Ralph.

"How is that show off?"

"Another first impression of mine, you are the prince and people do appear to simper and pander to your every request."

"And you don't?"

She rolled her eyes and answered, "Yes."

Brushing off the last of her tears with the hanky he had handed to her, Marg caught a whiff of his musky cologne and sighed, dreading the thought of leaving the comfortable warm arms.

Gosh, what is happening to me, becoming suddenly clingy like he is my man?

She kinda felt silly for having broken down in front of him. It was the stress, not that the almighty Garret would care at all in rescuing her from the fate of being Fletcher's daughter. If he were to ever voice out to her parents that she had ruined the date, she would likely be in trouble for it, in fact grounded for life despite being considered an adult.

All she wanted was to further her education, couldn't anyone answer that request of hers? Instead, her life had been reduced to dealing with overzealous men who thought her role was to be in the kitchen and the other room, the Simone's who wanted her to get fired and the Garrets who were still under the, can't figure you out category.

"Can we take a little walk," Garret asked once he stepped away and Marg slightly shivered from the loss of the warm body. Biting down hard on her lower lip, she reluctantly nodded. It's not like she had anything to do after Ralph gave her plenty of time to spend it with her 'fake boyfriend.'

"I gather you've taken a few acting gigs in the rejection of male suitors' arena," Garret remarked with a smile while Marg giggled at the way he put it. Garret frowned slightly, "I wonder if that's what you just did on our date."

Marg scoffed and rubbed her sweaty palms on the front of her uniform. "I don't like you Garret and I wasn't acting."

Clutching on his heart, he pulled a pained expression and whispered, "Ouch that hurts."

Right, like anything could ever hurt you.

"You can always say no to your parents," he advised, throwing back at her, the same reasoning she had offered a while ago.

Marg furiously eyed him instead and watched him smile again at her, before he grabbed her hand and they trotted a bit across the road to the other side. The street didn't have any traffic lights hence tended to be busy during the six to eight evening hours.

A cool breeze could be felt in the air; Garret took off his jacket and placed it over her shoulders, while Marg gratefully clutched at its warmth, sniffing in at the spicy fresh cologne before she looked at him in horror. Sighing in relief, she realized he hadn't noticed her involuntary action but was rather intent on leading her to the well-lit park.

"Psychology."

"Hmmm." Garret briefly looked her way. He sat down on the bench and Marg resignedly followed suit. Tucking her hands into the soft folds of his jacket pockets, she looked to the sky.

Night time had set in and instead of feeling tired like she would have at this hour, she felt refreshed.

"That's what I intended to study when I finished high school," she explained.

"What stopped you from doing so?"

Marg sadly shook her head. "My family feels it's a waste of time and that I should concentrate more on settling down. Margaret, all you should be focusing on, is making a favorable match and having babies. Your husband will take care of you and your children, that's what they usually say. My fate, reduced to that. Do I really need to be dependent on a man? Why can't I pursue my dreams then eventually settle down? My mom even suggested that my husband will educate me after I have given him the family he wants. The only reason why I took up the waitressing job in the first place was to save some money for varsity. Since no one is willing to help, then I would do this on my own."

Garret understandably nodded his head and felt a sense of admiration bludgeoning from deep within. She surely has guts, he thought.

"We appear to have something in common then," he said and watched Marg disbelievingly look at him. What, did she think that he was without problems of his own?

"I was serious when I said my mom had my date with Simone all lined up when I got home. Your family is like mine in one fact, early marriage. We Henderson's are meant to get married at eighteen. When you are way above that, it gets messy. You're suspected of being weird, a player and indecisive over what you want in life."

Marg smothered a laugh.

"How does one's decision making over what they want in life, get determined by whether they are married or not? Then we have the church, which encourages junior pastors to be married because as you're aware, women just love to throw themselves at an unsuspecting single, innocent junior pastor." This time Marg did laugh and to think she'd thought she had it bad.

"The reason why I was able to avoid all that talk before is because I immediately went to bible school after high school. Ever since I completed my studies, my mother has been at the forefront of presenting a horde of women to me. I try to say no, I really try," he sighed and pinched the bridge of his nose, "but it just doesn't cut it for me, since I find myself having agreed to yet another blind date."

Marg dabbed a few tears on the corner of her eyes from laughing at Garret's rueful expression. He liked her laugh.

"It's not funny. I can assure you, if you see some of the women, you will realize why I prefer you to them."

"Well, well pastor Gee; I wouldn't have pegged you for a snob."

"Ha, ha, very funny, here goes," he said and grinned at her. A flurry of butterflies she managed to squash out almost rose in her tummy.

"One lady asked me to pray for her. Reasonable request, I'm a pastor, so, it's to be assumed that when I go out on a date, prayer requests should follow."

Garret was turning out to be funny, with a dry sense of humor she liked.

"She says to me, she suspects that she has breast cancer. The reason why she would conclude that is because there's a lump, she feels on the right side of her breast. So, I raised my hands up to pray for her and to my shock, she took my hand, placed it on her breast and claimed that's how she was going to receive the anointing for her healing."

Marg burst out laughing again; she couldn't help it, especially with the horrified expression Garret wore at the end. Shaking her head in mirth, Marg thought about how the innocent pastor must have been traumatized by the experience, if that look was for real.

"Serious?"

"Yah serious, I was mortified. We were in a restaurant, not that I would have had such a private session at any given chance. I quickly withdrew my hand and made up an excuse before I left her in that restaurant, our supposedly date over and done with."

"The nerve," Marg said in between giggles. "My turn." She sniggered. "The guy who told you I was a prostitute, when I met him, he kept going on and on, on how many times he would take me once we were married. First date and he already acted like a teen on heat. So, I said, why don't we do it now? Which do you prefer, oral, anal or the real deal. You should have seen him make the fast trot to the door. I didn't hear from him again, but somehow, he managed to turn the tables and whisper to a few that I'm loose, which of course people who know me failed to believe." Marg winced at the statement while Garret laughed. He felt that he had met someone who was used to talking big yet didn't mean any of it, unlike the other women he had gone through so far.

"You are crude, you know that?"

Marg giggled and winked at him. "Isn't it odd though, that when this guy had been suggesting all that, I was meant to be the docile lady, take everything in like a sponge, no offense at someone planning out their long sessions of sexual fulfillment. But when I took charge, now it was a problem and I was the prostitute? This confirms my theory, in order to get rid of the riff raff, be extreme."

He chuckled. "I will keep that in mind for next time."

Marg shook her head in good humor, "Pastor Gee, don't try it. You might end up in a worse position," she advised while he grimaced and nodded. She did have a point, if he went extreme, either the whole scenario would be published in the papers and he would be called the perverse pastor or the women were bound to take it further.

"Another one feigned being possessed."

"Was she?"

Garret shook his head.

"What did you do?" Marg shifted on the bench and got comfortable before she cradled her chin in her hand. Garret cleared his throat and thought about how pretty she looked, really giving all her attention to him and focusing on the story at hand.

"She feigned feeling hot and started removing her clothes. My mother had invited her to the house and left us alone, so we got to know each other better. Once she started tugging at her shirt from the skirt's waistband, I knew I was in trouble. A grown assed man like me had to resort to calling their mother for help."

Tears of laughter were already running down Margaret's face as he narrated the story. "One look at her from my mother, had her sanity returning back, which proved she wasn't possessed. Mom accompanied her to the gate and watched her drive off. For that whole week, my mother didn't speak about marriage."

Marg dabbed the corner of her eyes with the hanky still trying to stop laughing and failing dismally.

"Why did you call out to your mom though?"

Garret scoffed. "If I had touched the woman to stop her from stripping, she would have screamed and said I compromised her." He pasted a cute grin that had Marg thinking of a naughty boy hidden beneath all that macho-ness.

"My mom was also meant to be witness to what I had been telling her pertaining to the daughters of the church and why I thought them not suitable. She figured I had been making excuses. They weren't as bad as I had described them."

"Ooh now I see. I am beginning to get why you wanted the one month. I didn't make those overt moves on you. I guess I seemed normal to you from the other blind dates."

Garret chuckled. "With the garish orange lipstick and that tent you had worn. You bet, not forgetting the quick temper and the "I don't care attitude."

She thoughtfully looked at him and whispered, "Guess I should have done those and we would not be here chatting like this."

"Margaret." A corked brow rose while she blushed. She was enjoying their talk and would have missed it if she had taken it to that extreme. She cringed at the thought of what she did to him to end their date. "Sorry about the water."

"Which water?"

Marg contritely looked at him. "The one on our date, and the second one with ice."

He shrugged. "Guess I deserved it. Next time I will have to avoid places with water," he winked while she laughed at the easy way, he appeared to be taking everything. Very much different from the strutting rooster she had pegged him to be.

A sudden thought of what he had said, drifted into mind and had her widening her eyes. "Wait a minute, are you trying to tell me that the things I had worn to put you off, actually worked against me."

Garret nodded, "my mom would have been delighted if she had met you, dressed like that. The perfect pastor's wife is what she would have termed you."

Marg gulped in a couple of breaths. "Are you serious?"

"Yep." A pause followed before Garret asked, "Alcoholic. Why would someone think that?"

An ice-cream vendor pulled up at the park and set up his business. Garret stood up then grabbed her hand and led her to the place.

What was up with this guy, over grabbing her without her permission? Marg sniggered at the thought since she happened to be enjoying it too much.

After selecting a flurry for himself and her favorite strawberry ice cream, Garret led her back to their bench and listened on to her explanation.

Marg scooped a spoonful and nearly moaned before she continued. "This guy came in for our date reeking of cigarettes like he literally bathed in them. He asked, which drink Marg. And I quickly answered, double shot whisky on the rocks, mix it up with gin and tonic. I mean I'm blindly pulling the drinks I hear people speak about, while my companion looks at me in horror. He went like, "Alcoholics are a no, no for me," and I threw in my two cents; "chain smokers don't care about their health and arc a no, no for me."

"You something else," Garret commented after his laughter had died down. They continued chatting about their bad blind dates. Garret felt like he hadn't laughed that much ever since he became a junior pastor at his church. Marg was funny.

Freezing for a slight second, Garett thought, how so like an old couple, after he exchanged his flurry with Margaret's strawberry ice cream.

Marg didn't appear to be fazed by the natural action, gladly ate the gooey cookie ice cream and winked at him after noticing the stare.

He cleared his throat, "Are you serious that your family has denied such a precious mind to be at varsity but rot in the kitchen?"

The thought that had set in his mind the first time he met her, drifted back.

Pretend. At least now he could be honest with her. Surprisingly during their first date, even though it was tense, he had felt there was a sweet interior underneath all that judgment, that's why he had dared her to date him for a month.

He cleared his throat while the little lady vigorously nodded at his statement.

"I don't know how you might take it, but I have an idea that could solve both of our problems."

Hope flared in her eyes, which she brushed off quickly by pasting a stern look instead. Garret grinned. Their little conversation at least had revealed that Marg didn't dislike him; rather she wanted to pursue her dream and be independent.

"I will sponsor your schooling."

She suspiciously gazed at him while he chuckled.

"On the other hand, you pretend to be my girlfriend. That'll make our parents stop breathing down our necks for some time."

"I don't see how that would solve the issue. I don't know about your mom but knowing mine, she will start stocking up on diapers and baby clothes the moment we announce we are together."

Garret shook his head. "You did mention your mom had indicated that your husband will be the one to take you to school. I can do that now while we date. There's the January intake at HC University currently going on. You can register with the rest and in a months' time you will be off to school. Both parents will be informed that we'll be speaking about wedding stuff once you are done with the degree. By that time, I figure you will be on your way to independence and I'll be having the perfect lady without the pressure of being rushed into marriage because of family or the church."

"What are you saying?"

Marg couldn't believe what she was hearing. Was Garret actually giving her the green leaf she had sort all along but couldn't find? With his plan, he will be off the table where crazy ladies were concerned while she pursued her dream.

"Fake dating for three years, that is quite a long time," she shook her head, skeptical that this would in any way work.

"Tell you what. If one of us meets someone suitable, he or she," Garret corked his brow at her before he continued, "would have to inform the other party about it. By the way, hadn't you said school and independence were your priority for now?"

Marg huffed while Garret grinned. "What do you think, Margaret Fletcher? Will you be my fake girlfriend? Let me also clear a preconceived notion of yours that all men are the same. Sweetie, I'm one of a kind," he finished with a wink while Marg settled to snorting in an un-lady-like manner, then reached out to the soggy hanky and wiped off the tears.

Gosh, she was a mess.

"I still think you are full of it. Your little addition on the flawless, beautiful proposal, says it all," Marg wagged her finger at him, before grasping his hand, that had reached out to help her after Garret stood up from the bench, then quickly let it go when she had her balance.

A slight shiver passed through her body at the sudden awareness of their closeness while her hormones mocked her.

Of course, this was what had made her dislike him instantly when she first got a glimpse of him. At that moment Garret Henderson first walked into the restaurant then pinned his eyes on her, leaving her out of breath, she had known she was attracted to him.

No wonder her jealousy after seeing him with Simone. She was in danger of becoming like all the ladies who had prepositioned him.

Shutting her eyes briefly, she wondered how she would survive pretending to be his girl for three freaking years.

"Marg."

Opening her eyes quickly, she stared guiltily at the handsome man, at the same time with the hope that he hadn't read where her mind had wandered off to. Certainly not in the temporary arena where she was meant to be.

"Deal," Garret asked her.

A slight unsure smile tugged at the corner of her lips, which Garrett took as a consent.

"How do we seal it, hug or spit on our hands and shake on it."

"Ew! That's gross." Marg said with a giggle. Garret was funny. There was so much to this junior pastor she knew she was yet to uncover in the three years.

"A simple handshake will do," she said and stretched out her hand. "Deal."

"First duty as your pretend boyfriend," he joked while she nervously giggled. "Let me take you home." Instead of letting go of her hand, he merely turned so he held her properly and smiled at her. Exhaling slowly, she could feel the quivers start all over again while she walked by his side.

Was she serious in that she would survive their little arrangement and remain the way she has always been? Untouched and relentless towards her goal.

Garret seemed to be unaware of her confused thoughts, hence it gave her a boost of confidence, as they slowly made their way back to the hotel to collect her things before he took her home.

Chapter 4

Four words in total, "Honeys in five minutes," before Garret hung up the phone. Margaret stared at her phone in confusion. Did Garret just summon her?

Oh hell, he did. She frowned and nearly stamped her feet in irritation.

"Margaret, if you want to make it early for your morning duty, you better go home and rest," Ralph advised her before he walked away from the staff locker room.

Grinding her teeth in exasperation while watching his retreating back and sticking invisible needles into it, Marg asked herself what was the use of Cathy having him for a boyfriend, if he didn't give her best friend a break?

She had been trying to negotiate for her duties since she wasn't that much of a morning person. The duty roaster for the next two weeks required her to turn up to work in the morning. Yolanda had agreed to swap with her but Ralph was being impossible as usual. Apparently, he figured their conversation was over after her handsome boyfriend decided to call at the same moment, she was in the middle of doing her one-man protest.

Audibly exhaling her breath, Marg reached to her lacy black jacket in the locker and put a semblance of order on her hair. Garret would have to meet her messy—raggedly, tired-self, having not given her the opportunity to freshen up.

He was back to being the stiff prince as she had concluded him to be, the first time their eyes locked. Walking out to the entrance and logging off from duty with her name card, she thought about how she would skin him alive for being demanding on their first day of officially being a fake couple.

Especially after she hadn't spoken with him for the freaking whole day. Her pride had detected that he reached out to her first and the more her day went by without him doing so, the more irritated she had become.

Infuriating man, she mumbled underneath her breath as she walked to her car. Her insurance was about to lapse and her twin brothers were yet to send her the monthly allowance they usually gave her.

Why did the world have to be so full of men who only thought about themselves?

She drove to Honeys still miffed with all the men in her life, her father, brothers, Ralph and not forgetting the insufferable fake boyfriend Garret Henderson, the new addition to the list of her woes.

Wasn't it a bit late for a pastor to be meeting up with his girlfriend?

What if he tried something funny?

Pressing sharply on the brakes and the car coming to a halt at the parking lot, Marg cautioned, stop being silly, mumbling the words beneath her breath.

Garret is not taken with you like you are him.

While her hormones had suddenly come alive yesterday, he was the same person she had met a few hours back. A bit on the friendly side, she grudgingly conceded.

Besides, Honeys was a twenty-four-hour restaurant unlike their hotel restaurant which shut down at 9:30pm, he wouldn't try anything funny with all those late comers around.

Thinking about the horrified expression he had pasted on, at the recollection of his blind dates, she giggled. An innocent is what Garret was, unlike her brothers. She couldn't imagine Godfrey and Leonard, looking at the hooked fish and going like, nah, not interested. Despite them being happily married to beautiful women, they had a share of their side chicks and would have gladly included the lady into that fold.

Yuk. She had seen too much smooching from her elder brothers with their so-called girlfriends, to last her a lifetime.

Schooling her expression into a semblance of a smile, she failed dismally and settled for a scowl instead as she walked to the table where her beau sat waiting for her.

Garret looked to the door and abruptly stood up once he spotted Marg. Her expression said it all, she was mighty pissed and about to create a scene.

He hadn't given her much of a choice, considering the women smiling at him while seated at the table on the far end, he nearly scowled too. He had better things to be doing, like jotting out a few notes for the Sunday service, than seated here to appease a parent.

Before Marg could yell at him, he grabbed her hand, taking her momentarily by surprise and engulfed her in a hug, then whispered near her ear, "Hi honey, you can get angry with me after, right now we're being watched."

Marg seemed to freeze for a second and to his relief, responded to the hug. Inhaling the flowery scent that clung to her, he summoned an image of a bible verse, than faced the fact that Marg made his senses reel.

Shifting and pulling away before he got carried away from something as simple as a hug and Marg ran for cover when it dawned on her that he was aroused, he turned her to face the two women in both their lives, his mother and her aunt.

"Your mother and my aunt, together, yay!" she whispered breathlessly while Garret chuckled. Funny, he thought. Their first date was bound to be exciting. The women might write a story of them to dish out to the family like Garret and Marg were the hero and heroine in their families for the time being, before they latched onto another unsuspecting member and arranged a blind date for them.

Greg was bound to be pissed off when he realized his brother hadn't been able to hold off their mom for long.

The women merely waved at them before they continued chatting like they didn't exist. Garret snorted; he knew his mother well enough. Considering when he had called Marg, she and Margaret's aunt were standing next to him in his office at church, before they dragged him to Honey's.

"Don't be fooled," he whispered to Marg, "they are watching us like hawks."

Marg whirled to face him and snorted before plopping on the seat.

"Definitely didn't expect that. You should have given me a hint." She stared at him with accusation in her eyes.

A corked brow rose. "I did. My tone said it all, desperate, I need help. Mom has been breathing down my neck since I told her yesterday that our date went well and I wanted to see more of you."

"You call that desperation. Henderson, you bloody summoned me here. That was not desperation but a command that couldn't be disobeyed."

"Margie sweetie you exaggerate," he said dismissively while Marg resisted the rise of the butterflies in her tummy at the endearment and failed dismally to stay impervious after that warm hug.

If Garret hadn't shifted, she would have remained in the strong arms and her aunt would have definitely married them off in an instant.

I can do stern and unaffected like the mighty hunk seated across me, Marg thought and watched Garret place an order to the waiter.

"Want anything?"

She shook her head. "Water is fine."

He corked his brow again before he nodded to the waiter.

"I'm not sulking. I've already had dinner."

"Ok," Garret simply said while Marg huffed. Like she had mentioned, their workplace had plenty of food, it was surprising she hadn't gained a bit after she started working there.

The waiter came back with the chocolate lava cake and her silly tongue had to salivate while she cleared her throat and opened her bottled water before pouring the contents into the glass.

Garret took a spoonful of the cake, Marg literally held her breath at the gooey chocolate liquid released from the scoop. He looked up to her and winked before he ate it. Shutting his eyes in appreciation, she felt like she should be moaning in delight too. Really, was he going to be doing that for the next few minutes, torturing her beyond measure?

Scooping more, he brought the spoon to her mouth. Her eyes widened.

"I know you want it. Your aunt was willing to tell me a few secrets of yours before you arrived."

"Sell out," she snorted, then gladly ate. Oh God this is so good, she thought as Garret fed her more.

Could she say she had indirectly kissed him, considering they were sharing the same cutlery?

They continued eating and probably making the two adults beat themselves over with pride for having brought them together.

"You can relax, they are gone," Garret advised after her last bite, in between moans she had managed to release from the joy derived from the gooey chocolate.

Marg looked back to the table and as Garret had mentioned, the women were indeed gone.

"Phew, that's a relief," she mumbled and leaned back on the chair.

"Honey I also didn't want to be here," Garret mildly said, knocking her off with his attitude.

For a second she had thought he used their families as an excuse, seeing he could surely pull the smitten look, which had made her toes curl while he was feeding her.

Bummer.

"At least we agree on that fact, we both don't like this," she retorted back, pressing down the voice that said in her mind, she was blatantly lying to herself.

"But it can't be avoided," Garret added. "Unless you want to back down." A challenge is what he was issuing and she was game.

Frowning at him, the thought of her dream going through her fingers had her shaking her head vigorously before she ground out, "Not at all sweetie. The goal is what I intend to achieve."

Garret laughed. He changed the subject by stating, "The mewling sounds you were making had me thinking of other things."

By the way she reacted to his statement, Garret smothered a laugh. He could settle for a surprised Margaret at any given time and not angry Marg with a permanent scowl.

Marg gasped; she couldn't believe he had actually said that.

"You sounded like one about to sell their soul for the next bite of the cake. Didn't you say you were fine; water was what you wanted? To my surprise your eyes glossed over and I was forced to give you a bite, since those weepy eyes were bound to make me not have the full pleasure of my treat."

Marg giggled at the description, at least he didn't say she was drooling on the table like a Labrador; hot chocolate lava cakes were her Achilles heel and her aunt had definitely sold her out.

"For a second I thought you would say I sounded more like I was being strangled while a man had passionate love with me."

As to be expected, it was now Garret's turn to be shocked. He frowned and raised his index finger, "Marg behave. We should go over some ground rules while we pretend to be dating." Spelling the ground rules out with the flick of his lean fingers he continued, "You will minimize on your colorful language, floozies, love making and all that sex talk, it isn't my thing babes. I don't subscribe to the BDSM stuff of pain for joy. Strangled while you were being made love to," he snorted at the same time shook his head before he continued, "You will avail yourself to me when I need a date, during family gatherings and so will I to you. Tomorrow we are traveling to HCU so you can register and while at it, we will look for appropriate accommodation."

Margaret scoffed at how stiff he sounded. Sanctimonious actually like a pastor, geez, he was one.

Garret was beginning to look more like her jailor. What if her past was shocking people, had she suddenly entered a prison by agreeing to all this?

Wait a minute, her ears perked, did he say they were going to Hillcrest University?

"What is it Marg," Garret asked when she raised a finger.

Licking her suddenly dry lips, she hoped what she was about to ask would not ruin everything.

"If I were to not agree to any of your suggestions, does it mean Hillcrest is off the table?"

"You do have a right to reject what I've just suggested Margaret."

Marg suspiciously stared at him. Garret had come to know that look within a day. Didn't she trust anyone?

Garret crossed his arms over his chest. "I will not withdraw my financing because you refused to act like the lady I gather you can be."

Margaret rolled her eyes on that note.

"One thing you will have to learn fast about me is that I keep my promises."

"No catch."

Garret found himself laughing. "No catch Margaret, although I would appreciate it a bit if you kept my mother off my back. If I was just your sponsor and you didn't pretend to be my girlfriend, it would mean, the women will be back and the blind dates will not end until I make a choice."

She giggled. He made his mother sound like a matchmaking monster with tentacles that never ceased to prod until they got the result they wished.

"As for the traveling arrangements, you still have two weeks to go before the deadline for the registration. You can go next week, except I won't be available, too busy with church things if you get my drift."

Marg bit hard on her lip. Wow, this guy was so considerate; she was about to really fall for him.

"Would you like to do this on your own?" He took out his wallet and placed the gold card on the table, which momentarily blinded her and took away her speech. Was he King Solomon with all his gold and a lack of what to do with it?

"I swear Marg, you can trust that I am helping you out because I want to, deal or no deal."

"Thanks Garret, I would appreciate it, if you were with me through this whole process." Clasping his hand and squeezing it for comfort, Marg smiled in delight, "I can't believe this is happening?"

Garret chuckled and placed his other warm hand over hers. For a second, they stared deeply into each other's eyes. Marg snatched her hand and looked away while Garret cleared his throat.

"One problem, my supervisor—," she said after having hoisted back her erratic emotions.

"No need," Garret waved his hand dismissively, "I spoke with him while you were on your way here, you are free for the next two days."

Just like that her woes had been put to bed in an instant. Incredulously, she asked, "How did you manage to convince him to let go of me when a while ago I was trying to convince him to move me to the afternoon shift to no avail."

Garret shrugged his shoulders and grinned, "I do have my minions after all."

"That will be presumptuous of me to want to kiss you right?"

"Margaret," Garret grumbled while she giggled and blushed at the same time. Truth be told, she felt like kissing him, out of gratitude of course.

Yesterday when Garret voiced out his idea, she didn't believe that it would pen out. Looks like things would move fast from here after. Who could have thought that the imperious handsome man with the piercing gaze would change her world in less than forty-eight hours?

"Shall we," Garret asked. Marg gladly stood up from her chair, then they walked out of the restaurant. She pointed to where she was parked.

"I will see you bright and early, tomorrow," Garret whispered near her ear after she squealed again and hugged him, having failed to hold in her excitement and not caring how he would react. For this once, she would relish the hug since this was her way of showing him how grateful she was for having met him.

Audibly laughing, Garret wrapped his arms on her, while she inhaled the spicy cologne. He sure had an expensive taste.

Garret watched her get into the car after they pulled away. Marg peeked out of the window once she got into her car, still beaming from ear to ear. She had the dreamy look that for a second managed to disarm him and almost make him feel like superman.

"I take back every evil thought I had about you when I was coming here. You are now my prince charming," she happily hollered then waved him off while he shook his head.

He was in trouble; he thought where she was concerned. He hoped he wouldn't lose his heart to her, while they played this game of keeping their parents and their mechanization at bay.

Marg laughed at the joke that Mr. Henderson had made while Garrett had the audacity to wink at her and have her heart aflutter. They had been 'pretending' dating for five days now. As to be expected the trip to the university appeared to have worked wonders on their relationship too.

Marg had been like an excited kid with a bag full of candy throughout the whole process.

Garret already had a list of apartments near the campus that they were meant to view after her registration.

She settled for a huge room, cutely partitioned with a tiny kitchenette, living area with a fireplace and of course the bedroom. They even tried out the feel of the queen-sized bed.

Before you get ahead of yourself, they were both like one meter apart when they tried it out.

"You don't know what this means to me," Marg whispered to Garret between her sniffles. Gosh she really was a mess when it came to the whole emotional stuff. It was after they had slumped in exhaustion on the bed. A dip of the mattress as Garret shifted and merely reached out to brush the tears off her face with his thumb followed, while he thought about the survey he had carried out ever since he heard about Margaret's problem.

The women he had met, more or less came from monied backgrounds hence parents stressed more on education and starting their own businesses. He had thought Marg's story was an exception, only to discover the more one went down the ladder to the common man, education wasn't valued in the least.

It was a shock to him. The Henderson might stress marriage at an early age but they didn't stop anyone in any way from achieving their goals. For goodness' sake his two aunts Caroline and Juanita were part of the board of directors in Henderson Construction and owned other businesses on the side.

Marg informed her mom at the last moment fearing she would thwart her efforts and expose her farce. She more or less gave her a run down that she was now dating Garret and they would be traveling to

HC University. As to be expected, her mom suspiciously stared at her after the announcement.

"Relax ma, you did say my husband."

"He's not yet your husband and he's already sending you off to school. I know your aunt had mentioned that he's a good man, but is it wise to travel with him when you barely know him and for him to take such a huge role? What if you meet another person at school that you like more than him?"

Marg rolled her eyes. "In no way will that happen. Ma, I like Garret. I know it's too early to tell but still I think he is the best."

Her mom reluctantly agreed to her trip. "I will only inform your dad and the family if his intentions are made clear either through your aunt or to me." That's how their conversation ended, to Margaret's confusion.

And there she had thought her mother would be happy that she was doing what she wanted for her to do, in the first place. Settle down, even if this was going to happen after she completed her studies.

While she got ready for the trip, she had a laugh when she went to her mom's room and found her not there, but glimpsed a catalog of baby wear on her bed and knitting pins in a ball of yarn on the rocking chair. Her mom was probably preparing for the grandchildren on a sly even though having pretended to not accept the news.

Then there was the issue of another excited mother. Garret gave her a heads up that his mom would reach out to her. She didn't believe it. On their way to Crescentville, Lucille called to invite her for dinner at the farm.

Garret winked at her after the call ended, since Marg had put the phone on loud, before he turned on the music while he drove them to the airport.

"Expect a food hamper of every craving you might experience during your pregnancy," Garret joked while she blushed. Then she felt a smidgen of guilt over the fact that a lot of people were bound to be hurt from this. This was like the beginning of two families, bonding and blending to become one.

Two days down the line after their trip to Crescent Ville, she was now at the huge Henderson farm house and she had come to some sort of bargain with Ralph on interchanging the two shifts instead of holding one shift for the whole two weeks at work, which gave her plenty of time to be Garrets' stand in girlfriend as arranged.

"My son informed me about your intention to study further, how are the preparations coming along?" Garret's dad asked.

Marg gushed. "Great. Thanks to Garret, I managed to register for the January intake, secure accommodation near the campus and also get the required materials for the course."

Mr. Henderson smiled before he looked at Garret and asked, "What do you think son, will she make for a good therapist?"

Garret chewed at his meat thoughtfully and then replied after swallowing it. "Marg is a bad judge of character. She definitely needs education on the human mind. She might learn to be less judgmental."

Marg gasped at his answer and pinched his arm. "That's not fair," she retorted while the parents laughed at the young couples' antics.

The youngest son, who hadn't said much over dinner, abruptly stood up from the chair and excused himself from the table before he walked out of the dining room and house.

Garret nodded to the mother who had curiously looked at Greg's retreating back. Sliding his chair away, he got up and whispered to Marg that he would be back before he followed his brother.

"Greg must be disturbed over the new development," Mrs. Henderson explained.

Marg nodded her head. Not that she understood the closeness between siblings since she was the only one apart from the half siblings who always managed to get on her nerves. "You should understand that Garret and Gregory have always been inseparable. A third mix in the picture might have him thinking that he's about to lose his best friend—more chicken." Mrs. Henderson motioned to the casserole.

"No thank you. I am not able to take another bite of your delicious dish. My tummy is stuffed for the whole year."

Garret's mom giggled at her reply.

"Greg," Garret called out to his little brother when he got out of the house. He adjusted his eyes. Greg was staring into the sky while leaning over the railing on the porch.

"Are you ok squirt?" Garret asked and squeezed his shoulder in comfort before he settled down on one of the chairs on the porch.

"Ya."

"Need a beer?" He popped open his bottle while Greg stared at him in disbelief and retorted, "I'm only fifteen." He had picked up the bottles in the kitchen before he came out of the house.

"Hmm, wouldn't have guessed at all. You have these muscles popping out of nowhere which girls are beginning to get crazy over. Ginger ale for you then," Garret continued and opened the other bottle for his little bro.

Greg pasted the lopsided grin that everyone knew could only be pulled by him. Reaching out to the cold soda, he sat down on the other seat and took a sip. "Carrying barrels of hay for dad does that. He is a slave driver after all," he quipped.

Garret definitely knew that, since his dad was always on the side of making sure that every male in the family maintained his masculinity.

"So, this thing with Marg, is it serious?" Greg asked him.

"Mmm, I don't know squirt. I like Marg, I think she is cool despite not going to our church, coming from a dysfunctional family and being crazy cool unlike the girls at our church who are suspects when it comes to the whole chaste thing."

Greg laughed. "She is perfect then."

Greg chuckled again at the thought that he once warned Garret over the crazy teens in their church but his big brother didn't believe him. Guess ever since he came from the seminary, he has had his own share of women throwing themselves at him for him to consider one who didn't attend their church.

That's why he and his friends had decided to stay chaste till they got married. The world out there was an inferno with lust consumed youths.

After a long, comfortable silence in which both the brothers were taking sips of their drinks, Greg asked, "Have you told her yet..."

Garret knew what Greg meant, so he shook his head before he added, "At some point I'll have to tell her, when what we have gets serious." A sudden thought had him chuckling softly while Greg curiously looked at him.

"Marg thinks I'm a player, who will never settle for one woman and be faithful to her."

"Are you serious?"

"Yep."

"Wow. I never would have guessed or even concluded that."

Garret frowned, "you are my brother. That's why you think I am a saint instead of being like Lucas."

Greg laughed. Aunt Caroline who happened to be Luc's mom was often heard stating that her son acted like the spawn of hell. He sure loved women and women loved him.

"Tsk tsk,tsk," Greg shook his head. "Wait until Marg finds out how straightlaced you are and that you are a one-woman person. She will be disappointed, old man."

"Hey," Garret retorted, pulling at Greg's ear in the process. "I said she's crazy but not that crazy."

"Uh huh."

"Sorry I couldn't hold off being single till I turned thirty."

Greg narrowed his eyes after he managed to extricate his tender ear from his brother. "It's okay, I knew mom would force your hand into getting into a relationship before you turned twenty-five. The

Henderson folks are also breathing down her neck. It's the church on one hand and the family on the other, at least I have a few months to go until my sixteenth birthday, so I definitely have to enjoy this freedom. Once I turn sixteen, she will be on my case. How is a sixteen-year-old expected to get serious in matters of love?" Greg asked with a pained look which Garret laughed at.

"Have you told paw-paw yet about your plan not to be saddled with a wife at eighteen but to open your jazz club once your trust fund comes through?"

Greg shook his head. "Am still working on a water tight business proposal, that would have him giving me the go ahead before grandma says, when is our young Henderson settling down."

Garret chuckled at the same time marveling at his young brother. Greg was something else. When Greg was six and Garret twelve, their grandfather gifted them with two-layer hens each. Garret ate the eggs and the chickens were barbecued over hot coals of fire for thanksgiving dinner. Greg sold the eggs and bought more layers. Three little words from their paw-paw were uttered after the incident. Eater and Sower. That's how the fate of what they would do in life was determined. Garret would be under his father's wing and train for ministry while Greg got mentored by their grandfather in business.

"I like Marg and I hope things work out for the both of you. Let's get back into the house. I'm sure by now she must be horrified at having mom showing her our baby things, which will be passed to your children and mine."

Greg got up from the chair and started walking back into the house. A sudden thought of a picture of his four-year-old self, butt naked and being hosed down with water from the mud he had managed to smear all over his body in his naughty days, had Garret abruptly standing up and leaving his beer he had been enjoying a while ago before, pushing past his young brother and taking the stairs two strides at one go. He could hear Greg laughing at his expense.

Chapter 5

"Ho, ho, ho merry Christmas," Garrett said, adopting Santa Claus's voice while Margaret marveled at his suit. It was Christmas and a helluva of a day since from the time her eyes had popped open, it had been full of activity.

Actually, her two weeks had been full of activity ever since she added a new man into her life. The shift change was beginning to hurt too, and she wished that she had been warned before, of the influx of holidayers coming to their sweet little town and dropping by the restaurant in their numbers, whether it was morning or afternoon, somehow it all seemed the same.

She had to deal with buying gifts for her brothers and her pretend relationship was on the high rise, since she and Garret couldn't claim to be dating without meeting each other for a drink or heard chatting over the phone for a few hours as normal love birds, yuk. At the same time, her mom still suspected that she was up to no good as usual. Lucky her, to not have her mother's trust. Their plan would be the death of the both of them. Somehow, they had to put up a good front to their moms, and Marg was beginning to think she was liking Garret, this time definitely not out of gratitude like she had thought before.

What was there not to like?

He appeared not to impose on her but took what she would suggest to heart, while with her family she was used to being told what to do by her father and brothers without any thought on how she felt about the matter. Their word was the law that she had to abide by.

Like Garret had mentioned, his week was busy more than hers if she could admit. She wondered though, nothing was complicated at her church, that would keep a man busy for the whole day. On Christmas it was usually, the morning service being attended, Christmas play, Christmas carols afterwards and bye, bye, everyone goes home. With her curiosity piqued, she wiggled an invite from Garret and was set to go to his church and not hers.

Before she did that, she managed to give some of her half siblings who had come home for the holidays a gift each as they did the same per family tradition. How she didn't like it. As usual she had received the worst gifts which were not to her taste at all. Like the atrocious gold earrings from her big brother Bill, that had tiny feathers. Was Bill insinuating that she had the makings of a great drag queen?

Oh and there was the gift from Cliff, a skimpy bright colored dress that didn't leave much to the imagination. His excuse, heard ma, say you might end up a spinster since you haven't started dating yet. Maybe if you wear that, men will swarm to you like bees. Very funny.

Considering the time and effort she always put in their gifts, couldn't her brothers return the favor at least for once, by just giving her good gifts. Gosh it was so depressing. She sighed. After the gifting ceremony, she left for church.

Her sweet mom had winked at her and told her to make sure she came home with an engagement ring. Really ma, she had only been dating Garrett for two weeks. As usual her mom had gifted her with a pretty dress which she called the question popping dress and showed off her tiny, curvy figure to perfection.

Her mom claimed the dress would have Garret drooling and Marg was likely to receive an engagement ring because of it. Men loved what they saw, they were eyeball species to a fault, so with the little flesh Marg managed to show, the junior pastor would not realize what had hit him until it was too late for him to back down once he did.

Marg giggled at the thought of Garret being confused. Geez, her mom was surely not aware of the cool and always composed man she was dating.

What she hadn't anticipated was the shock she would go through when she finally arrived at Garret's church. Her mom was right. It was about time she put her books away. The huge impressive building and many congregants had her gasping out of breath while his words rang back to her. I'm a role model to the youths at my church.

Oh, he was one of those Pastor's kids. The ones with mega churches, yikes. That cozy family dinner she was invited to a week before, didn't prepare her for this.

Now they were in the huge hall, Garret having changed from his impeccable suit to a Santa suit, before he started distributing gifts to the children.

Greg had given her fried spicy chicken wings in a paper plate then pointed out to the buffet, in case she felt like she needed more.

His mom welcomed her with a huge smile and warm hug when she saw her, then started moving around and checking if everything was going as planned. His father had waved at her before he continued talking to the older men of the church while they barbecued the meat. Such a busy family, Marg thought and she wished for Cathy to have been there with her. Cathy had visited her grandparents over Christmas.

"Uncle Gee, Santa uncle," three children who appeared to be almost the same age called and rushed to Garret.

"Marg," Garret motioned to her without turning. What, did the man have a bug on her, like he knew where she stood, watching him like a stalker, debating on whether to have good or bad intentions.

She walked towards him as he swiftly picked the squealing children one at a time and tossed them in the air.

"These are my naughty nieces."

The oldest who seemed to be around six, puckered her cute lips at him. "Elsie, Nita and Wendy."

"Hi," she brightly greeted. Another aspect she appeared to fail dismally at, getting along with children.

The cute girls merely looked at her like they were sizing her up and turned to their uncle. At that age, they surely knew how to dismiss a person, reminding her so much of her father's wives. She almost laughed. To them she didn't exist. They were proud of their boys while she was just Beulah's help, cruel right.

"Where's your mom?" Garret asked them. Elsie answered, "At the farmhouse, sleeping. Says she is tired from the journey."

Garret nodded and frowned, hoping that Aggy wasn't pregnant again.

"Their mom Agatha is married to my cousin brother Lucas Cooper," he explained to Marg. He had introduced her to some of his relations and she had joked over the fact that their families were both huge.

Marg searched in her mind where she had shelved the family structure of the Henderson's. Right, Cooper. Caroline Henderson, the fourth born to Matthew and Evelyne Henderson. Then there was Juanita, two ladies in the family among five or was it six males, she scrubbed off the list in her mind still keeping her eyes on the cute girls.

"What's with the kids' net," she asked as she watched the girls rush to their friends before they ran to Greg who was dressed like Santa too.

She nearly jumped when she felt Garrets gloved hand on her waist before he whispered,

"Let's just say Agatha, like every Henderson family member, has been indoctrinated into the baby making business."

Inhaling sharply as Garret pulled her slightly closer and her mind became mush, back to the goo, goo, ga, ga's parents used on their children. She despaired at her quivering body and how she was failing to breathe. Even with a gloved hand, the touch managed to sear her skin and brand her.

She wondered how his kiss would feel, if his slight touch and hugs had her reeling like crazy. Then her mom thought she was bound to fall for someone once she went to varsity. She resisted the urge to roll her eyes at the absurd thought.

Clearing her throat and slightly shifting to stare at him properly, she sweetly asked, "Will I be expected to do that?"

Her fake boyfriend who had pulled down the beard grinned. "No honey, I wouldn't expect that of you. Three is enough."

"You do know that I'm one of me right," she joked.

"Come-on let's go join Greg and his misfits," he said and grabbed her hand before he led her to his young brother.

Some old women who sat on the benches in the huge hall, sipping at the cool sodas raised a few eyebrows at noticing the body language going on between their young pastor and the beautiful girl.

One of them cleared her throat when the mother walked past them, carrying a few wrapped boxes. "Um Lucille, a minute please."

The pastor's wife smiled and approached them.

"Lucille, were you aware that Garret came with a lady to church?"

Lucille looked at them in confusion, since Garett was the one who drove the whole family to church. Her confusion cleared when her eyes fell on Marg and she smiled. "Oh, you mean Margaret Fletcher. She is Garret's friend."

Johanna stiffened on the side with outrage whilst her sister Freda Johnson scoffed. "Friend, hmm. Should our young pastor be entertaining a girl who is not a member of our church? Is he not supposed to be looking for a woman to settle down with, seeing he's now done with school? Plenty of our girls are still single, so it will not be hard for him to find the perfect mate."

Lucille chuckled softly. "These are questions that he can answer for himself, he is old enough. I should give these away," she motioned to the gifts, smiled at the two sisters and walked away.

"You see double standards," Johanna Johnson who had been quiet all along commented with a huff. "They encourage our youths to marry within the church while their own sons search outside." She wanted to speak further pertaining to the girl but decided to hold her peace until they got home.

Chapter 6

"Earth to Marg." Garret waved his gloved hand at her and she smiled. They were seated on the swings, sipping cold sodas while they breathed in the cool fresh air. It was official; Garret and Greg had the most infectious energy than she would have comprehended.

She had found herself loosening up and enjoying it, with the kids while they danced and goofed around. The Santa's were definitely energetic bouncy kids who had her breathing in huge gasps for air.

Garret and Greg had removed their beards and hats, and Marg was kind enough to wipe the sweat off Garret's forehead with a towel before they went outside to the swings.

"Ouch," Garret clutched his fake stuffed tummy. "Remind me next time that I'm no longer fifteen."

She giggled. Producing a red wrapped tiny gift, Garret whispered, "Merry Christmas to you Margaret."

"Garrett, you shouldn't have." She warily eyed the size of the box and thought herself silly for taking her mom's words to heart.

By the way, in case her heart had forgotten, she still wanted her independence first before she thought about settling down.

"Open it."

Producing a wobbly smile and slowly unwrapping the gift, Marg gasped in wonder and picked the delicate necklace with a triangle cut diamond pendant.

"It's beautiful," she breathlessly whispered. She wasn't a jewelry lover but at one glimpse of the simple necklace when she spotted it a week ago at the jewelry shop next to Honeys, she was hooked.

She had looked in dismay at the list of gifts she was still yet to buy, and her modest income before wearily sighing and moving on with her shopping.

"Can I," Garrett motioned to her and she nodded then shifted on the swing so Garret could have better access to her neck.

A slight movement indicated that he was getting rid of the gloves before he reached out to the necklace in her hand and slid it on her neck.

Marg adjusted the pendant to be between the cleft of her breasts while she inhaled sharply at the brush of his cool fingers on her skin.

Get a grip of yourself, Marg thought to herself, briefly shutting her eyes and imagining his lips taking over from where his fingers had left.

Garret dropped his hands and Marg turned to face him. "Beautiful and simple like you."

A flicker of an emotion passed through his eyes that Marg didn't want to analyze.

"I'm sorry," she guiltily stared at him. "I didn't get anything for you."

"It's ok," he chuckled while she beat herself up. He took her hand instead and said, "your being here with me right now, is more special than anything you can imagine."

Marg squeezed his hand and her heart did a somersault. Was she, no she wouldn't? Could it be possible that in two weeks she was falling in love with him? Abruptly standing up from the swing at the absurd thought, Garret stood up too.

"Is there something wrong," he asked concerned.

"Not at all, I just got the feeling that someone is poking a few pins in a miniature version of me."

"What makes you think that?" he asked with a laugh.

"Don't stare; just pretend to be looking past them. I think those grannies over there are watching us." She had spotted them staring at her while she had been in the hall too. Not that she was going to point out that fact to Garret.

Garret narrowed his eyes. Like Marg had mentioned, they were the center of attention, no wonder she thought someone was sticking needles in her body, those glares could literally be felt from where they stood.

"Do you want us to go back inside?"

"Nah, I am not a chicken. I can brave it. I wonder what they are saying though, something like, how dare she, who does she think she is, hanging around our junior pastor while our daughters remain single."

Garret threw back his head and laughed.

Marg took his hand and beamed at him while he wondered what she was up to. It wouldn't be good. She was extreme after all. "I think we should take a bit of a stroll towards them, and speak about how you will marinate me tonight.

Garret couldn't help but clutch at his side. "You know Marg, you are terrible."

She really wasn't going to listen to him pertaining to toning down on her colorful language.

He could as well imagine the Johnson sisters experiencing mild attacks at hearing that kind of talk being said in the ears of their sweet junior pastor.

"By the way, I noticed a lot of young couples." Marg commented while at the same time she scrubbed the thought on how her hormones were screaming near Santa. Holding hands wasn't meant to be like this. Who was she kidding, ever since he shook her hand the first time, her palms appeared to get all excited and weep with sweat. In her conclusion, she wasn't meant to be near him in any way, since her body responded no matter what. She was deeply aware of him. Thank God, her school days were closer than ever and she would think properly without him messing up her well thought up plans for her future.

"The elders of the church encourage the youths to marry early, eighteen years being the minimum. They figure if one gets married young, they have the chance not only to nurture their children but instill good values on the third and fourth generations since they will still be alive and the wisdom that they have will be of great help when problems arise eventually. A lot of things can be avoided too, like sexual immorality. The more one remains single while they date around, the more they are likely to fall into temptation."

"Does that ever work?"

He nodded. "Our divorce rate is low and most of the youths haven't experienced and ventured into deeper waters so they essentially have fulfilling sex lives once they are married." He shrugged, "you can't desire for sex outside when what you know is honorable and truthful since from the first go, sexual intimacies were confined to the marital bed."

"So, you mean you—," she eyed him curiously like one looking at an alien for the first time. Garret crossed his arms, "I what Marg?"

Blushing profusely at the question and lowering her eyes so he wouldn't see the curiosity in them, Marg snorted, "never mind."

Garret leaned in and whispered, "Yes Margaret Fletcher, I haven't been with a woman."

Oh boy, virgin man walking, she was going to faint. Furiously fanning her face, she thought this was definitely what she would have prayed for if she wasn't so keen in being independent, a man the total opposite of her father. After having witnessed the wives fight for her father's attention, she just didn't have the strength for it.

Garret's faith would ensure he never pursued another woman until she died. Her doctor brothers might have married one wife each, as an act to not follow in their father's footsteps but still had a horde of mistresses on the side. She knew that all those shenanigans would abruptly end if they were to be accountable to someone higher than them.

To her, love was meant to be shared between a husband and wife and the couple had a lifetime to discover and know each other better. If God had felt that the two people He created first would know each other instantly, hence be bored with each other for eternity, He would have created them, Adam, Eve and Mary or Eve, Adam and Steve. Their world was really wacko and screwed, she thought.

That's another reason why she had stuck to her books and not dated like some of her friends, since she had figured if she couldn't get that man, then books would be her solace. In no way would she share her husband like her mother.

Garret chuckled and asked her, "Have you?"

Her eyes widened as she retorted, "never. I'm yet to receive my first kiss."

Garret laughed while she huffed and stamped her feet. "It's not funny."

He leaned in and touched her forehead while she blushed in embarrassment. It was now his turn to view her like an alien from outer space. "Such big words that always manage to come out from such a tiny person, who hasn't experienced any of the things she says. Wow Marg."

She pinched his arm.

"Ouch—" he shifted his hand before he concluded and had her beaming in delight from the compliment. "On a serious note, you should be proud of yourself. It's a great accomplishment actually." Now that was more like it. She would definitely simper under that praise.

"By the way with all that said and done," Garret slightly frowned. "Doctor Margaret Fletcher, please explain to me then, why from the same pool of good girls who are being taught over and over again the same teachings in the church, have I met the crazy ones who want to show me more and age me before my time."

Marg winked at him, a graying Garret would still not be bad at all. His father was still a handsome man after all.

"That's easy to figure out. You are the junior pastor of a megachurch. You come from an influential family. You are handsome, charming and very considerate. If they can't make you see them, then they really have to make you see them."

Garret grinned. "How come all those attributes aren't working on you baby."

Resisting the flurry of butterflies that rose again in her tummy from the way he was looking at her, Marg stood akimbo and retorted, "Ten handsome brothers who think they are God's gift to women and one conceited dad, who can't let a beautiful girl pass him by, is why."

"Did you just place me under the same brand as your family members because of my looks again." Before Marg could reply, Greg walked up to them and grabbed her hand.

"I think you have hogged Marg long enough for a day. She needs to meet other people too."

"Who are those people," Garret growled, not yet finished with his girlfriend, while Greg's grin widened like he knew his older brother was taken in with his beautiful, spunky girlfriend.

"Your best friends of course."

"Wait a minute; I thought Garret was a loner."

"He is, they are my best friends but he butts into their lives and says his opinions like they are his."

Marg giggled, that she knew so well, since he butted into her life too.

"Are you coming," Greg asked Garret and he resignedly followed them.

"Are you sure these kids are fifteen," Marg whispered to Garret who had now changed and for the first time was wearing jeans and a shirt. Yikes the man surely had strong arms.

"Yep. Brad is the youngest. Ethan is the only one who is actually seventeen." The handsome teen Garret pointed out to her, had an afro, thick hair that would have made any woman run for their money just to have it.

"Don't tell me you are now itching to plait his hair," Garret whispered and she swatted his arm in outrage.

She curiously looked at Ethan while he talked to Greg, taking note of a few hand gestures she would have considered feminine. She tilted her head to Garret. He smiled and winked. "He is not." Was the simple answer he gave to the question in her eyes.

"The suit," she pointed at it. All of them were actually wearing suits apart from Greg and Garret. If she were to be asked to comment about Greg's friends the first thing she was bound to mention is that they were tall, sophisticated young men who didn't look their age and who were definitely going through a suit fashion frenzy. Close to them she actually felt dwarfed. Such handsome young men who didn't seem to be aware of how the other young girls kept on casting coy eyes at them, to grab their attention.

"Our suits are made by him."

"Whaa—," Garret clasped his hand over her mouth.

"You are loud, you know that." She huffed before he took his hand away.

"How is it possible? I thought they were imported?"

Garret laughed. "He's a designer. In a few years' time, he will get famous. I feel it in my bones."

Now it was her turn to laugh. Garret was right though, if the seventeen-year-old Ethan Ross was the face behind such stylish suits, a great future lay ahead of him.

"Let me get this right, we have the finance advisor Greg, the designer Ethan."

Marg had asked Garret on why he chose to be a pastor on their journey to school hence he told her the chicken layer story.

Apparently, his young brother had a business acumen that had one thinking of stealing him and placing him in a genie bottle. He then added that he actually loved what he did. The decision for him to be a pastor might have been made by his grandfather and determined also by the fact that he was the first male son to Graham Henderson hence would take over after him when he eventually retired, but Garret knew beyond doubt, God had called him to this.

"The IT guru Brad and as for Dominic I guess he is just Dom. Unlike the rest, he bounces and lands on his feet with whichever he chooses, like MacGyver."

Dominic Knight grinned at something Bradley said and she flagged her hands over her face at the grin. Player alert, she thought while she was fascinated at having met the heir to Knight Industries for the first time. Thanks to her twin brothers who loved the good life, the K1 luxury car Garret drove, which they each had, was part of the latest series of fleets made by the automobile company.

She snapped her fingers, "Which comes to my question. Are you pretty sure these boys are 15."

"Yes, they are 15."

"Hmm and all this time I had thought my brothers were impressive."

Garret laughed. "I mean my brothers have made strides in their professions before they hit the thirties. Godfrey, the first son of my dad's first wife, is now thirty-five and a neurosurgeon. There's Leonard, a cardiologist, he is thirty-three. As you can see my dad's first wife, Dorothy churned out doctors. She is mighty proud of them and doesn't seize to goad my mom about it. The second wife, Judy—."

Garret interjected, "the Fletcher boys. Those I know because of the youths who love their music, Gordon and Gifford."

Marg nodded, and of course she hated her half-brother's music. It made her feel like a sex symbol instead of a woman with feelings. Especially when their music videos more or less showed skimpily clad women.

"Do you?"

Garret huffed, "why would I like their kind of music." She shrugged. "Just checking."

He shook his head in mirth.

"Then from my mom it's just me. You would think from all that testosterone the family will be relieved that yay there's something feminine in their midst. Apparently, I'm not meant to dream. I should look pretty and marry well."

Garret snorted.

"There's Denzel from dads fourth marriage, he is 27."

"Wait a minute, you are in third and you are 18."

Marg giggled; Garret would soon become confused with her family dynamics like she was of his.

"Ok, so dad married mom after she was his mistress for a year. As you are aware, she was an exotic dancer. When he married her, his head had become cotton candy from all her body and leg shaking and in the heat of the moment he was like, you are my one and only, no more women. You have finished me. You're the queen of my heart, lady love, all that hogwash men use to get their way. In his defense, so my mom never left him for another man."

Garret laughed. Marg really had a sharp tongue. He frowned at the same time at the thought that her mom had told her all that. Should he be worried that Margaret might one day make moves on him that would have him lose his head?

Surprisingly even though having not met Beulah, she was legendary. He wondered what his mom had been thinking when she put Marg on the list of potentials. Dismissively shrugging his shoulders, he continued listening to her. Despite what others might say, Marg was a lovely girl who made him laugh.

"With her, he had finally found the one. My mom is a beautiful woman, just look at me, so she figured, I'm pretty special indeed, I've the great assets that have men drooling like Labradors and the sexy moves. How in hell will a man leave all this and look for more?"

Ok he had to admit, Marg was hurting his sides, he hadn't laughed this much in a long time.

"But you see, two vain people under one roof, is a recipe for disaster. Anyway, back to my story, my mom struggled to conceive; ten years down the line she had me. All the time she was living under a rock thinking she is the favorite only to discover when I was two that he had fathered other boys with another woman. Apparently while he comforted her in her failure to conceive, he was making babies with another woman at the same time. Who became his number four, when she decided enough of the hiding, hey Beulah I exist, you aren't the favorite but just one passing fancy."

"Your dad is something else." Garret huffed

"Tell me about it," she rolled her eyes. "That's Claudine; from her there is Denzel who is 27, a gourmet chef and Bill a pilot 25."

"Bill who?"

"Oh." She flagged her hand. "Bill used his mother's maiden name, Bill Lewis." Garret frowned and Marg for a second was taken aback. Did he know her brother? That was a silly question indeed; of course, it was possible he knew him. Pilot, duh.

"Are you ok?" She touched his arm. Garret stared at her and for a second, a chill passed through her body at the coldness she saw before he smiled and returned to his normal self.

"Continue," he said and motioned with his hands. "Really Garret, have you returned to being the master commanding his minions around."

He clutched her shoulders and smiled, "no sweety, you are certainly not my minion. Do continue."

She cautiously stared at him before she spoke of Cliff, but the excitement she had felt in telling him about her family had deflated. She smiled but all of a sudden felt numb in her emotions as a niggling sensation passed down her spine.

Greg grabbed her again before she could say more to Garret, dragging her away from him while he chided his brother to stop hogging her.

Did she say something wrong? she wondered, staring at the brooding man with arms over his broad chest, who looked proud, like one who didn't care about anyone else, very much different to the warm man she had come to know.

It was like he was now back to being the man she had met the first day they had their date, superior and aloof, not at all one who would do anything to please her, a mere mortal. She sadly sighed before she listened to Dominic and the story he was telling his friends.

Chapter 7

"Marg baby, your lover boy is here," her mother advised while she huffed and almost retorted. He is not my lover boy.

Ever since Christmas when Garret suddenly cold zoned her, he became busy. For six days she didn't see him. He did call her and chat briefly before he would be interrupted by something going on and would hang up.

Did she have a right to feel disheartened? Absolutely not. After all their relationship was fake, those were the words she clung to for dear life. Even though the first two weeks she spent in forced company with him, told her otherwise.

Instead of pining after her fake boyfriend, she was meant to be getting excited over the days flying by so she would be securely at school and away from the pressure of being forced to get married.

The six days she hadn't met up with him were not all that bad. The doctors came over for the holiday, laden with good gifts. Her car insurance cover was now in order all because of the twins. Men! She had huffed. All of them actually made sure that she had everything she needed, as in everything, but every time when she suggested varsity, it was always the same answer just like her mom, little sis, you need to get married. Ah huh.

We do not want any man messing you up. Surprisingly enough, they hadn't yet come across Garret and her mom was still being sneaky over the whole issue.

She could swear that maybe part of the fact that she never had a boyfriend at high school, apart from her wanting her independence, were her infuriating half-brothers.

Cathy was back in town. Marge had whined to her over Garret's behavior.

You are in love with him, Cathy had screamed, nearly bursting her eardrums. She denied that fact vehemently. Four weeks wasn't enough to form any attachments.

"Why is he here? He should have gone on living his life like I don't exist." she snorted and checked the time. It was 11:35 pm.

Tomorrow was the beginning of another year. Yippie. She got off the bed and stared at herself in the full-length mirror. Why would she freshen up for him anyways? She released an irritated breath, smothered the blue strapless doll dress and went downstairs to meet him.

"Hi," Garret stood up from the couch. The boy could surely wear the jeans in the same manner he did his suits, to perfection.

He had on a brown leather jacket over the ribbed black jeans and indigo t-shirt.

"Can we go out for a little drive?"

Marg nodded. She turned to her mother who was standing by the door.

"Make sure you bring her right on time Pastor Gee. She might be an adult but she is still my baby girl, so if she stays out more hours than appropriate, I will not hesitate to order you to keep her with you forever."

Ooh mom, Marg resisted the urge to roll her eyes. Garrett cleared his throat, "what time is most appropriate to you ma'am?"

"Ma'am, ooh, you do have a keeper here Marg. Before 3 am next year," she winked and watched them leave.

"I like your mom," Garret commented once they were outside. Or he liked her silky long legs in the tiny shorts she had been wearing. Her mom turned heads including young boys half her age. She looked at Garret who smiled without the evidence of lust in the depths of his eyes, like some men she knew, who usually pointed out that they would get the beauty from Fletcher. Slowly nodding her head, she slid into the car seat after he opened the door for her. They drove on for a couple of minutes in silence.

"We are here," Garret announced. Looking up, she realized he had driven to the famous bridge in their town, which looked like two open palms holding up the bridge on both ends. A few people were there too. Coming around to her side, he opened the door for her and held her hand as he led her to the bridge. Garret sighed. His sweet Marg looked sad and he knew he was the cause of it. He had been so wrapped up with preparing for the conference; he hadn't given her enough attention. That was not the only reason but still he couldn't help but feel responsible for hurting her.

He nearly chuckled. He was turning out to be a sucker for punishment. He had tried to resist her, but had failed dismally.

Apparently, he had fallen under her spell, according to the Johnson grannies who were not impressed with his conduct of late. He respected his elders hence left with his dignity intact despite the aspersion they had thrown at his relationship with Margaret. When he thought up the arrangement, he never anticipated another aspect, that some of the people in church would not take too kindly to him dating Fletcher's daughter. On the other hand, his mom was quick to assure him that all would return to normal. Wait until they found out three years down the line that this had all been a lie, hopefully they would be quick to forgive.

"Marg, is there something wrong?" he asked.

She huffed. "You are what's wrong. One minute you are cold and the next hot."

"Sorry love, I just had a lot of things on my mind. First weeks of the year are usually hectic. With the youths about to go to school, we have a youth conference in which we minister unto them the freedom we have in Christ. As you know schools are usually a hot spot for promiscuous behavior, children going wild because they have the freedom to do so. No parents breathing over their necks after all."

Margaret stifled a laugh.

"I see that smile." He slightly inclined his head and Marg found herself laughing, no longer angry or agitated.

Garret opened his mouth to say something, except the people who had also come out to watch the fireworks started counting down.

Ten, nine, eight, seven, six, five...

Marg excitedly joined in and smiled as Garret did the same. Fireworks burst forth in the sky; lighting up the night and making it feel like day. Happy New year! People hollered, others hugged, kissed, and wept whatever emotion could be racked out from having made it to the new dawn.

Gareth pulled her closer and Marg suddenly felt shy. He cradled her face and whispered. "Happy New year Margaret."

Damn, he really was attracted to this girl, Garret thought. Pretense or no pretense, this was his reality from the word go.

Marg smiled, "happy New year Garret," before she was pulled into that warm embrace that had nearly made her knees buckle under the first time. She deeply inhaled the spicy cologne, fresh as always, she thought while Garret whispered near her ear, raising a few hairs while at it, "Stay the same Marg. Sweet and kind. Please don't change."

Someone cleared their throat. Garret and Marg turned and they both gasped.

The famous musicians were quizzically looking at him, while he figured the older ones who could be the doctors, had arms crossed over their big broad chests.

Garret knew the twins were crazy since they had been stories of drug abuse too. It didn't surprise him at all when one of them said, "Godey, Leo, G2. Did I just see my little sis in the arms of a man?

I think I didn't, I must be going blind—I definitely must be going bliiind."

He paced further away, stretched his arms out like one groping in the dark before he looked at them, rubbed his forehead and shook his head. As usual, his jeans were lowered slightly while a few gold chains hung on his waist. Tattoos marked his arms and the other twin had dreadlocks thus distinguishing one from the other.

"Did you kiss her?" Gifford asked.

Garret would have laughed if it had been someone else facing up to Marg's brothers, but he knew better not to rattle the cage. He answered, "I didn't kiss her."

Gifford removed his shirt and stamped on it. Gordon, his twin, caught his arm.

"Relax," he said he didn't.

"What?"

"He didn't."

"Wait," he walked towards them and narrowed his eyes since Garret stood protectively in front of Marg.

Marg pouted her lips and shifted. "Guys you are embarrassing me."

"Wait, wait..." Gifford wagged his ringed fingers, not paying attention to his lil sister.

"Why haven't you kissed her hmm? Do you think she is not beautiful enough?"

Oh brother, Marg could be heard huffing.

The older brother who had been observing everything with a thoughtful look on his expression finally said, "Wait a minute." Godfrey pointed at Garret, "You are a Henderson, you good people." He broke into a broad smile before he pulled Garret and hugged him.

"Marg, be a good girl and let me take you home," Leo said. "We need a word with Henderson here. Don't worry sis, he will be in safe hands."

Marg was fuming and at the same time quivering in fear, so much for her mother who was yet to inform her husband about Marg's relationship. Now her brothers would beat Garret to a pulp.

Garret on the other hand seemed not to be bothered. He merely smiled at her and nodded while Leo pulled her towards his car.

"Guys you are not fair, mom is aware of us and Garret should be the one taking me back home."

"If it's like that, we will trail behind you till he drops you off, your ma, vouches what you just said then we have a little chat with him."

Marg fumed.

"Marg, it's fine," Garret said. "I'll be okay."

"No, it's not fine. Godfrey, go home to your wife and children and lecture them over the pitfalls of kissing. As for these drunken twins, please, please, take them to rehab."

"Are you sure you do not want to reconsider, I mean look at her, that tongue. She is a shrew that will suck you dry. Maybe that's the reason you haven't kissed her yet." Gordon cut in.

Marg screamed in frustration.

"Crazy right," Leo said before he picked her up, bodily put her in the car and drove off.

Chapter 8

The phone rang and Marg quickly grabbed it. Finally, the call she had been waiting for. After she got home, she couldn't help but threaten her brothers that if they hurt just one little hair of Garret, they would have to answer to her.

"Hi," Garret greeted, his deep voice coming clearly through the phone while she clutched at it as if for dear life.

"Oh God Garret, are you safe?"

He chuckled, "our conference is on, sorry I didn't get back to you sooner."

"My brothers, did they hurt you?"

"No Marg, your brothers are cool."

"Serious."

"Yes, seriously."

"When will I see you to ascertain proof of life? I almost dropped by your farm, you know."

Garret chuckled, "You wouldn't have found anyone, everyone is at church. I just called to inform you that I might be busy for a while."

"Ok, so my brothers and dear old dad did threaten you to stay away, right?"

"No Marg they didn't."

"So why is it that you don't want to meet?"

She could hear him wearily sigh. "Ok Marg, I will come over to your place every day for these remaining days before you leave for school, even if it's just for a second," he promised and he did just that.

He would come over in the evening, she rushes outside, then he would cradle her face and smile. Thank God their relationship was now in the open and no one appeared to be making snide comments in her family about it.

"I have seen you; I should go now," he would say after.

He certainly was crazy, she thought.

On her last day at home, the day before she went to school, she invited Cathy so they could attend the evening service at his church. That had actually been at her mom's suggestion, after she had whined to her that she saw less of Garret, now that the family was involved.

Her mom was quick to offer her advice in that if she wanted to be near Garret, then she got involved in his ministry. That was definitely not a good idea, because already she liked him to a fault. If she saw him at work and got close and personal with what he did, what would happen to her poor heart when this all came to an end?

She was right in time to see him walk up to the podium. Cathy winked at her. He wasn't wearing his usual tailor-made suits, but rather casual.

Black leather jacket, white t-shirt, blue jeans, ripped at the knees and black ankle boots.

"Is he going for the biker look?" Marg asked with a raised brow, while Cathy nudged her and coughed.

"We are in church, he is no longer your boyfriend but a minister of the word, so respect please."

She rolled her eyes at that.

Gareth said a few jokes, which had the youths in stitches. Then he preached on God's grace. Marg sat up on her chair. No longer did she see the biker clothes, no longer did she see the handsome young man who would laugh at her crude ways, but instead she heard the message coming clearly from his lips, very much simple that a five-year-old would even understand and have them scrambling to their Heavenly Father's lap, kissing Him with slobbery kisses because of the tangible love He had for them. It was the pure, unadulterated message of how the Father had reconciled Himself to the world in His Son, Jesus Christ and the call for the youths to awaken to that truth which was still echoing till to date.

Her world did turn around on its axis and she was faced by one single thought, standing right there on the podium and ministering to hundreds of youths was not her boyfriend but a man of God.

"Marg."

"Hmm," she came back to earth with a start while Cathy looked at her.

"The service has been over for about 20 minutes now, everyone is leaving."

Abruptly standing up, Cathy curiously looked at her with a slight concern in her huge expressive eyes. "Are you ok?"

Marg smiled. "Fine."

Cathy nodded then they walked out of the hall and Margaret spotted Garret's mom speaking to a couple of women before they left her side.

"Margaret," she stretched out her arms while Marg walked straight into them. "You've been scarce these days dear," his mom remarked and Marg giggled at her language. She pulled back and answered. "I have been quite busy, tying up the loose ends before I leave for school."

"Are you ready for the new adventure?"

"Yes definitely," she answered with a giggle.

His dad came over and remarked, "Here she is, the one who made Garret escape the service on New Year's Day."

Marg furiously blushed while the wife swatted his arm to stop making her future daughter in law uncomfortable.

"How have you been dear?"

"Good thank you," she replied with a nod. "He might take a while," his father commented after taking note of Garret who was surrounded by youths of around sixteen and early twenties.

His mom hugged her once again and whispered, "Don't be a stranger, dear" before they left for home.

Marg watched him, from where they had left her, standing in a daze and still trying to process the sledge hammer that had hit her during the service.

A few ladies approached him, including those who were older. He gave each his full attention, listened to their issues and prayed for some. Throughout she had been thinking of Garret the man and never the junior pastor. How did he manage it?

She looked at his face while he spoke with some young attractive ladies, he smiled but it was never in any way suggestive. From having witnessed her dad and brothers flirting, she knew the cues that gave them away if they had any interest in a woman. She didn't see that in him. He was courteous, calm and collected, not at all what she had thought before.

She cringed at the words she once uttered the first time she met him, having pegged him as a player.

Should she be elated that during the month they were together she had met and seen another side of him that those other ladies speaking to him were not aware of? That Pastor Garret Henderson could goof and joke around, be petty, irritated and cut off her smart mouth at times. Laugh at her bad jokes and be real with her, while making time to be with her despite a busy schedule.

What were those other girls thinking when they acted out for him, to not be aware that he was just one of those cool guys that one will always want to hang out with. A guy who wanted a person to be upfront with him from the word go.

He walked up to her and for a split second, she caught sight of a tired look cross his eyes before he looked up and brightly smiled at her.

"Hi sister Margaret Fletcher."

"Hi," she greeted back.

"Thank you for joining us today," he said with a wink while she smothered a laugh at noticing the grannies from last time, pausing in mid step to glare at the both of them.

Cathy came over to greet him, having drifted away from her to catch up with people she knew.

"Did you bring your car?" Garret asked her. She nodded.

"I will drive you. Let Cathy take your car." Marg thought of the miles to her home then to his home. She shook her head.

"There is no need for that."

"Marg." He corked his brow.

"Fine," she grumbled, then handed Cathy the keys before Cathy winked at her, hugged her and left them standing alone.

"Shall we?" he motioned with his hand.

She nodded as they came out of the huge building. Once she was in the car, he touched her sleeve. "Marg is everything ok?"

She nodded. They drove in silence, her tongue tied in knots since she didn't know what else to say to him.

Had she been so selfish, never caring enough to ask him how his day went?

What kind of girlfriend was she, not to realize the huge role he played at his church, while her family drama merely appeared to be exactly what it was, trivial? The family drama he had managed to put to bed once and for all after the bridge fiasco with her brothers.

Her new year had really arrived with a bang. That same day, her brothers confronted her mother and spilled the beans to their father about the new man in her life. As to be expected, Fletcher senior was quick to chortle in glee like a two-year-old receiving candy after hearing that his daughter had snagged for herself the most eligible bachelor in Harmony.

The other wives on the other hand were not impressed and were quick to point out that Marg must have used one or two skills on how to seduce a man to land him.

Beulah furiously defended her daughter's innocence to everyone in that she was a virgin then after they got inside their house; she was quick to ask if Marg still was.

Oh brother, Margaret had literally flapped her hands in exasperation and nearly died out of mortification when her usually sweet mom demanded to do the test. Dorothy also came to their suite of rooms to ascertain that fact.

She never told Garret about it. Garret was set to meet her dad in the afternoon. The afternoon when he had been meant to be at church with the youths.

When he finally did meet up with her dad and spoke to him, there was a shift. Whatever he might have said to him, must have made her father view her in another light since he announced afterwards that no one would throw any kind of aspersions over hers and Garret's relationship. Marg would leave for varsity to study psychology, whoever had an issue with that, would answer to him, and hence the grumbles were silenced in his house for good.

How she had longed to meet Garret then, except when she tried to get a hold of him, his phone wasn't available. When he called, relief washed over her and all she thought of when he told her he was busy with the conference was that he was now pulling away from her.

Despite that being a strain on him, Garret merely humored her, by dropping by her house to see her for a few minutes, go back to church then travel back to his home. In all that time Marg never thought of what she had just witnessed this day. That he was a pastor with a flock that needed him.

Finally, she slid off the seat once they got to her house.

"Good night," she mumbled and almost rushed away, except Garret's deep voice reached her ears and had her turning around to look at him in dismay.

"Tomorrow I am driving you to school."

"You can't."

"Why not?"

"Coz you are tired."

"Who says so?"

She wrung her hands. Snippets of conversations had drifted to where she had stood while she waited for him, on how he was so hands on with everything. Garret is the one who had proposed the youth conferences to be held before the teens went to school.

He looked to the wellbeing and development of the youths, not only by feeding them with the word, but making sure that during the day they participated in different activities to get the chance to mix and mingle. A few people had even lauded him for changing the behaviors and attitudes especially where delinquent teens were concerned.

And to think this was the same man who had been making time to meet her (his fake girlfriend) every day when he had so many things on his plate!

She nearly sobbed as it suddenly dawned that the one month of her changing her opinion about him had actually taken place.

He was nothing at all of what she had thought, proud, arrogant, and full of himself and a player. He was actually a giver and a man capable of loving her while she still maintained her individuality.

She should have been filled with dread when he proposed to sponsor her education that he might want to take advantage of her, because as the norm, men never did anything for free.

Instead, being his fake girlfriend had been like the most natural thing in the world, and Garret never took advantage of that. Her very brothers had been confident that Garret had preserved her innocence despite their mothers' insinuations.

Garret could sense her pulling away from him and he didn't like it one bit.

He walked to where Marg stood before he pulled her into his arms and whispered, "Remember what I said, don't change, remain you."

"I haven't," she pulled back and looked at him innocently, too innocent for that matter.

"I know that look, very well. Sweetie, I'm going to say a few things that you will need to understand very fast."

He pinched the bridge of his nose, and chuckled softly at her while Marg glowered at him for sounding stern with her. Drastic problems called for drastic solutions and he wasn't ready to lose a girlfriend because she had now built a monument on his behalf in that sweet tender heart of hers. He needed his spunky Marg, not the demure, quiet lady who appeared to be at a loss on what to do with him.

"Margaret Fletcher, there's only one who is perfect and He is above," he pointed to the sky.

"Whatever pedestal you have built for me here." He tapped her head, indicating her mind while she huffed in response. "Destroy it fast, overthrow and break it to smithereens because I am not perfect. I'm just a work in progress, just like everyone else."

He hugged her, taking his time as despair filled him up since her hands still remained on the side, until tentatively, like a bird coming to life and fluttering its wings, Marg returned his hug to his relief.

He almost said it then. I love you, Margaret Fletcher. In you I see not only a best friend but a mate for life. It was too early for that, so he settled for a kiss on the forehead and pulled away.

"Are we good?" he asked her anxiously.

Margaret smiled and nodded. "Good."

"See you tomorrow then, be ready by eight," he finished and walked away to his car, without taking a backward glance.

Chapter 9

"Will you be okay without me?" Margaret asked and ran her hands over Garret's broad shoulders. She had been in his warm embrace and was failing to leave the strong arms to go to her room.

Garret laughed, "I think I will survive. Girl you are so full of drama, so these next four months will be blissful and straight forward, not a ball of confusion that has been going on lately ever since you came into my life."

She pouted her cute lips at his answer. "You are so mean," she said. "You should admit though, that you haven't had this much fun," she winked while he chuckled.

"Yes Marg, I haven't."

They were standing in the parking lot, near her hostel. Garret as promised had arrived at her house at exactly 8 am to drive her to school. This time, he was literally her chauffeur and he had foregone the airport which meant they would have arrived earlier at the school.

She was fuming at the fact that he had taken over her life somehow, since seeing him there with her, happened to give her silly heart a glimmer of hope that she might mean something more to him than being his fake girlfriend.

How she so hated being clingy.

This was extreme. She could understand the financing part more than this side of things that managed to leave her in emotional turmoil.

When he had arrived in the morning, her mom accompanied her to the car before she hugged her once again, shedding a few tears while she did so.

"My baby girl is leaving the nest," she trilled in her sweet voice while Marg rolled her eyes and shut her eyes, so she didn't cry either.

Once she got into the luxurious car, and tried to clasp her seat belt on with trembling hands, Garret took one glance at the tears already making their way down her face, clasped her in the seat instead before he passed on a Kleenex from the box for the tears.

Marg looked back to where her mom still stood, looking like a lone figure. Her brothers traveled to their respective homes two days after the bridge incident. Her step mothers including her father, who had taken time off from his busy schedule, had wished her the best in the house before she came out with her mom.

The younger siblings, from her dad's fifth marriage, sons as to be expected had already stowed her luggage in Garret's car.

Cliff, the traitor more her age, who had gifted her with the skimpy dress was quick to give her a hug and whisper in her ear, "don't be falling for someone else at school after Garret has been through so much for you."

She had grabbed his ear whilst he squirmed.

"Are you trying to say I'm a light skirt?"

"Ouch, ouch, Marg I am sorry for having thought that. You are only devoted to Garret," he whispered before she let go of his poor ear.

She hugged and kissed his little brothers, Lucian 15, Donald, 12 and Edmund 8. Josephine was the only one who had broken the record by giving birth to four as compared to the two that appeared to be the norm.

She did ask Garret too over how he managed to convince her father to agree to her education. Garret claimed to have told him, Henderson women were holders of PhDs. So, if he wanted his daughter to marry in the family, he better allow Garret to do what he thought best for his future wife.

Very funny Garret.

"Do you think she will be fine?" she asked Garret as he drove off from their house, her eyes still glued on her mother. A warm hand snagged hers and squeezed it in comfort while she rubbed away the tears with the other which still held the tissue.

"She will be," he answered.

"I've never thought about it, but you know I have been my mom's world ever since I was born and now, she will be alone."

"Nah."

She huffed at his reply and Garret grinned, watching the road ahead. Her heart as usual fluttered.

"Your mom has Dorothy, Judy, Claudine and who is the other woman, that's too many women for one man."

Marg giggled. "Josephine."

"She has all those to entertain her. I bet now she will be telling them; my baby girl is off to school and is set to marry Harmony's finest."

"Really you just had to include yourself in the mix."

"Am a huge thing baby, so your mom is talking about her future son in law and my ears itch like hell."

She shook her head and slumped back on the seat; "you are terrible you know that."

Just like that, the miles passed up as they chatted and they even had the silent moments. She did doze too and was abruptly woken up to the blur of the music.

She had frowned at him.

"What, I am about to sleep behind the wheel all because my chatter box has gone silent," he said with a frown while she huffed and sat upright on the seat.

They stopped by a cozy restaurant, freshened up a bit and had a meal, then back on the move.

"Why?"

"Hmm."

"I mean why did you want to drive me? I could have traveled with Cathy than you having to do this. You must be tired from the conference."

"There you go again with your tiredness theory. Are you trying to push me away?"

"No, I am not, just curious on why you would put this much effort into a fake relationship?"

"Coz, I want to prolong the moment and be with you. Marg I'm in love with you."

A frown marred her beautiful features before she demanded, "stop the car."

"Marg."

She glared at him. "I knew it; you are just like the rest of the men, wanting something in return for the favors."

Garret stared at her in horror.

"Garret, why? Our relationship is fake after all?" Margaret asked.

Garret glanced at Marg, relieved that he had just imagined the whole scene playing out, about her getting mad at him for turning the tables over their fake relationship.

Marg had far much better things to be looking forward to now, her independence for that matter, and definitely wouldn't take kindly to one snatching her newly acquired freedom away from her.

He gulped down a few quick breaths, shifted on the seat and changed down the gear as he reached an intersection.

"I need to see you well settled, after all my money is in play," he joked.

"Right, you are my sponsor after all," Marge added with a smile that stopped short at reaching her eyes.

What had she expected really?

That he would tell her, he had fallen in love with her just like she realized yesterday that she was madly in love with him, while at the same time she'd berated herself that he wasn't for her.

He was just too perfect. That pedestal that Garret must have known she had erected in her mind when she saw him preach and minister to those youths was still there, clinging onto dear life.

Wait a minute, she still wanted her freedom right and not to be tied to a man?

Marg you are being silly, go and learn that's what's good for you now, she thought, failing dismally to scrub out the thought that Garret would not be by her side.

Finally, they reached her school and here she was inserting herself into the mix that he wouldn't live without her and failing to come out of his arms.

"Marg," Cathy screamed and rushed to her.

Marg reluctantly extricate herself from Garrets arms and hugged her best friend. Cathy was quick to motion to some boys passing their way to take her luggage. Marg raised her brow and Cathy giggled. "One of those perks of being a senior, fresh meat to do my bidding."

She turned to Garret, after her crazy friend left her for a while, to really say goodbye for the last time.

"I should go and get settled. Do you   " she hesitated, "want to come inside." She finished, thinking of the last time they were here together and they were beginning to get to know each other. It was so unbelievable that she had known Garret for just a month.

Garret shook his head and slid his hands into his jean pockets. So much she was still to learn about the man, considering the dark t-shirt tightly stretched over his arms showed part of a tattoo on his left arm. He had said it ran across his shoulder and part of his back, one of the silly decisions he had taken and made during his teenage years.

She wondered what kind of person he had been then and couldn't help but imagine him as a real, tough badass. The long-sleeved shirts and suits explained much. Garret wouldn't want youths thinking tattoos were an in thing even for pastors; hence try to imitate that, not knowing that those were scars of a person who had also had to go through God's saving grace, just like anyone else. No one was born saved, including the pastor's children; they had deep flaws and their own battles to fight.

Garret stared at Marg underneath his lashes. If he was to get into her room, away from prying eyes, he would definitely kiss her and that would be disastrous to their shaky relationship. One thing he was trying to avoid was scaring her out of her wits.

He would miss his drama queen, he thought.

Why did he have to look this good, Marg wailed in her mind? Those strong arms making her itch to be wrapped up in them, once again.

"I will see you around, hey."

Garret smiled. "Don't worry Marg, I will not forget you. I will call you every day so you don't have the time to miss me."

Her eyes widened and she snorted, "Who says I will miss you?"

"Come here," Garret said and opened up his arms. She ran into them, inhaling his dependable scent while he chuckled. "That reaction tells me you will baby girl. Failing to leave right."

She giggled, and lightly punched his chest. "You are failing to leave too. I swear, I am fine with it, if I don't see you for the next four months."

"Really, don't lie to me now." Garret tilted her head by the chin, looked deeply into her eyes while her breath hitched and she shut her eyes.

"Marg," he said. She opened her eyes. He was leaning close to her. Close enough to breathe in the sweet scent of the mints they had both shared and for their lips to brush. Close enough to see the emotions running in his eyes. The heat emanating from his body encompassed her in a cocoon and she nearly purred like a satiated feline, basking in the tender ministrations of its owner.

Cathy came back at that moment with some friends she had gone to high school with, Inocencia and Gina. She hollered, "hey you love birds, get it over with."

Garret cleared his throat and laughed while Marg felt like pinching her friend.

"I should go," Garret advised, hugging her again before he let her go.

Garret had walked a few steps away before he turned and seemed like he wanted to say something to her. Cathy dragged her off at that same instant and Marg was engulfed by hugs from Inno and Gina as they prattled on, over how she managed to convince her dad to let her attend varsity.

Marg groaned helplessly, watching the black K1, luxury car drive away before her attention was snagged back by her friends.

Chapter 10

If she had expected a snail's pace in her first month, she was to be proven wrong. She quickly adjusted to Varsity life and the endless rushing for lectures while she met the worst of the worst of the lecturers. You know those ones who always want to make life difficult for the students for no apparent reason.

They were actually a succession of them and she wondered if they had been churned out from the same varsity to make them act in that way.

Apart from that, she enjoyed the whole experience and she realized she had chosen the perfect program for herself.

On Fridays, she usually went out with the girls to some parties hosted around the different hostels and Sundays made sure she was at church.

With a fake pastor boyfriend, her spiritual life had to stay in shape too.

True to his word, Garett called her every day and they would chat for endless hours over nothing and everything. She missed him so much and had even contemplated going home for a visit, especially as V-day drew close.

Then she had really thought about it, and realized she was being unreasonable.

Kelly, Simone's cousin, had approached her in the library to invite her for a sleepover party. With nothing to do, having completed her assignment, she agreed.

She hadn't heard from Garret in almost four days now, and had assumed he was busy as he was prone. Even though her mind had been plaguing her in that, he might have found someone else. Four days was freaking too much to be busy. She very well knew, four days of absence from her father meant he had another mistress.

"Hey Marg did you see this?" Kelly asked her and handed the phone to her, while they walked towards her room where she would change before they met up with the rest of the girls.

"Flowers?" Marg asked, "What about them?"

She was confused on why Kelly would show her a bunch of random red roses, like she had suddenly become psychic and she knew what they meant.

"Uhm Simone says they are an early Valentine gift from Garret."

Marg brows rose.

"I'm serious, check out the comment on her fb."

"From my better half, GH," Marg read aloud.

"Who is GH apart from Garret Henderson? He is the only one with those initials that she knows."

Kelly pasted that infuriating smug smile while Marg could hear the blood rush to her ears, deafening any words that Kelly spoke after. She was right after all, four days of absence did mean something.

"Umm, sorry Kells. I just thought about a few pointers that I didn't add in my assignment. You can go ahead to the party. Let me deal with school first." She chuckled softly while Kelly looked at her in disbelief. Unlocking the door to her room, she smiled at Kelly who was still standing in the corridor before firmly shutting the door behind her.

That went well, Kelly commented below her breath after Marg shut the door behind her before she answered the phone.

"How did it go?" Simone asked.

"The girl looked quite stricken." Simone could be heard laughing in glee from the other end of the line. "By the way, why am I doing this?"

Kelly asked. Her cousin snorted. "I mean it Simone, what if Garret does come for a visit, then what?"

"Nah, nothing like that will happen. According to his secretary, he will be busy since he has to attend a pastor's seminar on the other side of the country. He will need to be superman to get there then attend the important seminar. Besides, one way or the other, the relationship is doomed. The elders in the church are not impressed and will be having a talk with Garret soon. I can't wait for my baby to come back to me and apologize. I will forget about this whole Marg thing in an instant."

Kelly giggled on that note and walked away to join the rest of the girls for the party. With Marg not being the center of attention since Cathy always pointed out her relationship with the handsome pastor, it was likely to be more fun.

Could Garret have started dating Simone? Marg wearily sighed and slumped on the chair in the bedroom.

Before his four-day disappearance, he had been acting rather distant as he appeared to be distracted whenever she spoke with him over the phone.

Her heart hurt like hell but she had agreed to all this in the first place. When did the lines blur between what was true and what was fake?

She thought of the last day when she saw him, the day he accompanied her to school. He looked like he wanted to say something to her. As days passed by and he never said, she figured it wasn't serious. Could it have been that?

She failed dismally to go through the already perfect assignment and sighed in frustration.

When she was meant to be partying with the other girls, living her life independently, this is what she had been reduced to; pining after a man who might not even want her, the same way she did him. Her phone vibrated on the desk.

"Hey sweetie," Garret greeted and for a second her silly body thrilled at the endearment.

"Hey you."

"What's up for tomorrow?"

Did he just call her to gloss over the fact that he now had an official woman, which meant she would no longer be having a fake boyfriend? She looked at her phone in confusion before placing it back on her ear.

"Is there something meant to be up?"

Garret laughed that deep, seductive laugh that always managed to make her toes curl.

"Nothing Marg. Just nothing at all. Can you just give me a rundown of what you will be up to tomorrow."

"Why should I?" she petulantly asked

"Margie baby, my parents are watching me like a hawk as we speak. Be a doll, honey and tell me your plans."

She huffed, then recited her schedule. Before he could say anything more, she hung up on him and threw the phone on the bed with a slight huff from her lips.

The parents must have been the ones who had made him call her. If it had been up to him, he wouldn't have. He would have been busy speaking to his actual girlfriend Simone. Wait a minute, what if Garret was to announce to his family that his arrangement with her had been all a farce. Then that would mean no more sponsorship for her. Augh, she pulled at her hair in frustration and hit her head lightly over the desk.

Bummer, she thought. All her well thought up plans down the drain, because no girlfriend of his would allow him to sponsor another woman.

She didn't sleep a wink. How could she when her precious future depended on the tossing and turning rounds she made on the bed. By the time she finished her last lesson for the day and was off to lunch, her head ached like crazy and she was contemplating sleeping after lunch.

She tightly grasped at the strings of her backpack, not in the mood to look at the girls around campus, squealing in delight and receiving their Valentine gifts from their boyfriends.

Cathy had taken one look at her and retreated. A dark cloud had sat on her that said it all, stay away.

"Marg, wait up," Walter called her before he ran towards her. "What do you think?" He shoved the bunch of white lilies to her face, forcing her to let go of the straps and hold them instead. Inhaling the sweet scent, Walter asked her, "Do you think Inocencia will like them. I know it's a tradition that people give away red roses."

Walter had a roaring crush on Innu, while he wasn't aware that Innu nursed the same crush for him. Marg smiled. "White lilies are her favorite. This is a thoughtful gift; she will love them."

"Phew, you don't know what that means to me Marg. What about you? What did you get on this special day? Kelly is glossing over her cousin dating Henderson, and telling everyone that you lied about being his girl."

Marg sought for comfort by inhaling the sweet scent of lilies. She never spoke about her relationship with Garret by the way. Her best friend is the one to blame for this whole mess. Her fight with snooty Kelly over her snobbish cousin had Cathy blurting out that Henderson was dating Marg and ever since the December holiday.

"I guess I'm a bloody liar," she mumbled and came to a stop when her companion, on the side, abruptly stopped walking. Looking up to Walter, she swept her eyes to where he was staring at and nearly fell flat out since her legs suddenly became weak.

Leaning at the bonnet of his E class Merc Benz was none other than her handsome fake boyfriend. He was immaculately dressed as usual, with no hair out of place in his gray tailor-made suit, broody looking, and fresh to be sampled on.

Garrett's eyes traveled to her hands that were still clutching the white lilies and from where she stood, she could recognize that narrowed gaze that said it all. He wasn't impressed. She guiltily shoved them back to the owner and nervously chuckled. "Umm Walter see you later. Innu will be smiling and pasting kisses on your face if you hurry with those."

She turned away from him and started walking towards Garret, wiping the sweat from her palms at the sides of her jeans.

By the way, why was she nervous? It's not like she had committed any crime to be ashamed of. Theirs was a fake relationship and they had agreed to tell the other personally if one got involved with anyone else. A point she forgot about yesterday, when Kelly showed her Simone's Facebook page.

His gaze didn't waver from her, but he stood there looking superior as always, while if he had minions, they would certainly have been scrambling around him.

"Hi," she slightly pulled her curled hair and rubbed at her brow.

"Hi to you," Garret replied, still not in any way looking away from her. A few students appeared to pause a bit with wide eyes as recognition dawned on them. Her mom was right; she certainly had lived under a rock, not to have been aware of the Henderson and their popularity.

"Come here," Garret commanded when she failed to take the last steps to him. She huffed, patronizing as always, what happened to the sweet guy who she hung out with over Christmas. She frowned.

"Come here Marg. Your boyfriend must be waiting for you, so let's do this quickly, and get it over with," he raised a brow and looked back past her. Walter hadn't moved but was still watching them.

"He is not—," she snapped her mouth shut. Why would she explain herself to him? She faced him, head-on as the implication of what he had just said hit her. Stamping her feet in irritation, she retorted, "Garret Henderson, I am not the two-timing person like—," she didn't finish because Garret had already closed the gap between them, cradled her head before he swooped in and kissed her. Surprise, surprise, her body screamed at the delicious onslaught.

Chapter 11

"Oh my, who is that?" Cathy asked, nudging Kelly who was clutching at the box of chocolate and sniffing the roses she had received from her boyfriend. More like demanded from him if he intended to remain her man. She looked up to where Cathy was pointing to, at the parking lot.

She narrowed her eyes and gasped. "No, it can't be, my cousin—."

"Ya right," Cathy cut her off with a snort. "Your cousin can't be dating that man who is all over my friend."

"The junior pastor doesn't do PDAs," Kelly fumed, "maybe it's his young brother."

"Right and I had thought they were just two in his family. His little brother is still in high school. As for pastors showing public displays of affection, I guess that makes them human after all." Cathy giggled while Kelly huffed, stamped her feet picking up the scattered pride and walked away.

Cathy was enjoying the show. It's about time, she thought, her best having told her about the fake relationship, this was as real as it could get. She reached for her phone and took a snapshot before flapping her hands like crazy and hollering, Finally, you go girl.

"Is there someone urging us on, did she just say finally," Garret asked as Marg smiled and played with his ear before kissing him again. "Long story."

He chuckled and drew her for another kiss that left her reeling. It was a surprise that she could still stand, considering her legs had turned into jelly. Or maybe it was Garret's firm hands on her, as she was wantonly pressed against him that were offering her that support. Like she had imagined before, his kiss had branded her for life. She was ruined for any other man.

"Wow, this is a huge surprise," she mumbled. His eyes widened before he slightly pushed her away.

"Hey, you made me do this. Pastors don't show their affections in this manner." He placed his palms over his car and whined, "We are meant to be exemplary." Then she thought those Korean dramas were terrible. She rolled her eyes and crossed her hands over her breasts. Ok, sensitivity there. If only her mom had warned her that their bodies once they went hot, it would take time to cool off.

"Really Garret?"

He winked at her before he grabbed her hand and pulled her back into his strong arms. Oh, boy.

"How did I do?"

She happily smiled. "Perfect."

"You are fine with this right." He was pasting sweet little kisses on her face while he talked. She snuggled up, relishing every sweet kiss and touch.

"Fine with what?"

"Taking the three hundred and sixty degrees turns over our relationship."

She frowned at a sudden thought and pulled away. She needed the clarification before she fell head in first to her doom. "What about Simone?" she asked.

"What about Simone?" he stared at her in confusion. "Is it about the roses?" Margaret's heart sank when he said that. So, it was true.

Garret shifted from her, walked to the car and opened the back door before he motioned her to him.

Bouquets of red roses were lined up on the back seat. She gasped in shock. "These are for you. I placed an order yesterday at Marilyn's flower shop and informed her I will get the fresh roses early in the morning. A weepy Simone called me at night, crying over the fact that they were no longer any left. Apparently, all flower shops had sold out of roses and the last batch at Marilyn's had been purchased by me. You know how I do not like the water works; I advised Marilyn to give her one bouquet. Did you notice, is it that clear that one is missing." He scratched his chin.

Marg couldn't help but laugh. Was he being serious? "What do you mean missing?"

"I had bought a bouquet representing the sixteen dates we had before you came to school. Because I gave one to Simone, there are now fifteen." Then he grinned, with the expression that said. Sorry babes about that but I will do better next time.

Marg laughed. How could a man be so endearing? He was turning out to be very different than she had thought. He had done everything for her and this sweet gesture had her wondering. Could he be like some pastors she had heard of? Garret seemed like one who loved to spend money, did it mean congregants... Before she could run wild with the thought, she heard some girls chuckling behind them.

"Yep, that is definitely Garrett Henderson, owner of Honeys."

Her eyes widened. As in Honeys her favorite spot where they usually met after their first date.

"Earth to Marg. Warrap."

"Honeys," she raised her hand in confusion.

"Ooh that. Long story. It's one of those business ventures my thirteen-year-old brother made me get into once I turned eighteen and my trust money came out."

"You said one; does it mean you have more?"

He shrugged his shoulders dismissively. "Let's just say. I have a good financial advisor."

"Who the hell are you people, thirteen and eighteen huh?"

Marg knew that despite being eighteen and going for nineteen, she was still dependent on her parents while others appeared to be making more money than she could imagine at her age.

Garret loved the cute expressions she was making. Marg his drama queen. A deep sense of possessiveness had him grinning as he pulled her back for another kiss, not able to resist the full soft lips that responded to him with the same fervor he felt. Every guy at campus was meant to stay off her radar from now on, including the Lily guy.

He would make sure he made her aware of how special she was to him, that she would not have the insecurities she harbored which he was aware of, which she had voiced out a couple of times. She really did think all men were like her family.

Having grown up and witnessed the love his parents had for each other, made him aware that everything was a choice. Geez, his paw-paw and granny still blushed like teens and teased each other before they would kiss. Whoever said love faded with time, lied. His grandparents were a strong force to be reckoned with and at the forefront of advising their grandchildren to stay chaste until they said the I do's.

He looked to the hands clutching the lapels knowing his immaculate suit was creased during the kiss while Marg made the mewling sounds that had him thinking of other things, not in any way noble as was expected of him.

He will definitely marry her and very soon he thought before he drew away.

"To answer your question sweet Marg, I'm just a simple junior pastor at a small."

"Not small, mega," she retorted.

"OK, suit yourself, mega church in Harmony, who happens to be fathomless in love with you Margaret Fletcher."

"Really?"

"Yes, really Marg. I loved you from the first moment we met."

She pulled back. "Liar."

He chuckled, "oh God, I didn't like you at all. Especially with your snobby attitude."

She huffed.

"Do you think you were any better? Glaring beneath those dark lashes like you had minions waiting around to do your bidding."

He pulled her back into his arms. "And then," he interrupted, "I got used to the real you, the sweet girl with a zeal to break out from the norm and boundaries that have been set over her life. I really liked that girl. The more I got to know her, the more she went under my skin. She was demanding too, proof of life, serious. Are your brothers the Mafia or what?"

She squirmed and pinched his strong arms.

"Marg, I love you. I, Garrett Henderson, am crazy about you." He finished soberly while she looked at him, with wide eyes at a loss for words.

"I know that expression," he chuckled. "Only you Marg. You are my one and only girl. Don't bank on me having another one, you will be sorely disappointed."

She huffed. He did know her insecurities to a hilt.

"How can you be so confident? People do fall in and out of love."

"Yes, if they think love is an involuntary action that they can't resist, brought about by a half clothed tiny angel with a bow and arrow."

She giggled and traced his strong jaw with her finger.

"Honey, I have made this choice to love you and only you. Till death do us apart, that is if you agree to marry me when I eventually ask you. For the meantime though, I'd rather you fulfilled your dream first."

"Wait a minute, are you proposing that you will still wait for me?"

Garret nodded while her heart hammered in her breasts. What if she couldn't wait, would she dare tell him that?

Nah, Garret was too much of a gentleman to be thinking of tearing her clothes off her back, like she had been imagining of late. She gulped in a few quick breaths and bravely smiled at the fact that apparently pastor Gee had seen his wife in her, considering he wasn't dawdling about and stating he needed to see if they were compatible enough before he married her.

Garret held her hand. "Come on; let's go on our first official date." Marg squealed and let him open the door for her. She couldn't wait to also tell him how she felt about him after their date, even though it was evident from the way she had responded. For the meantime, she was still glossing over the fact that the perfect man was now her official boyfriend.

"Hey Marg," Cathy greeted and sat next to her on the bench. They were in the canteen the next day after Valentine's Day. Her day had been wonderful afterwards with Garret.

"By the way missy, where did you go for your date?"

"The Imperial hotel, why do you ask?"

"So, they are right?" Cathy frowned.

"Right about what?" Marg stared at her best friend in confusion.

"Rumor has it that you lost it yesterday."

"Lost what?"

Cathy stared at her in exasperation. She motioned with her fingers.

Marg huffed. "He is a pastor."

"And a man too. Handsome, virile young man," Cathy added. Yep, she could vouch for that, having seen the passion in his eyes and the tenderness he held her with, promising that they would not get carried away. As much as she loved him, that area was to be experienced once they got married.

Marg giggled at her friend.

"You did it!" Cathy's eyes had widened like saucers.

"No, I didn't dummy. We dressed up in our nines, went out for dinner, a movie after then back to the hotel."

"Then—," her friends' eyes were sparkling and she could guess her ears itching to hear more details.

"We binged on kdramas then fell asleep in each other's arms. Today I got ready for school; he dropped me off and left."

"That's it?"

"Yep, as it turns out, he is attending a pastor's seminar on his dad's behalf, hence dropped by to celebrate V-day with me after he was informed the dates had been slightly shifted."

Cathy snorted, "That's it."

"Yes, that's it, was something more meant to happen?"

"Augh, and I thought I would live vicariously through you and you will tell me that you did it and how wonderful it was. Ya, Ya," she flagged her hand before Marg could speak.

"He is a pastor, an extraordinary one I guess who can resist your charm and you are still bloody virgin Mary."

Marg giggled. "You are funny. I think mom will be shocked too if she ever got wind that I spent the night with him and nothing happened. She will say Margie baby, it's impossible. Men are relentless and will never lie next to you without getting their own share of the cake and eating it. No matter how angry I am with your father, he knows while I am still drowsy with sleep, I can't resist him. Yuk right."

Cathy giggled as she recalled how horrified she was when Marg finally invited her to her house on her sixteenth birthday. They had known each other ever since they were twelve but Marg seemed to be embarrassed over social calls to her home. The mansion was impressive to her on the outside while Marg pointed out that it was because a couple of suits had been made for each wife to stay with their children, that's why it was huge. Apart from that, they were just a middle-class family, making ends meet.

Cathy was soon to discover the other embarrassing fact of her cheerful, sweet friend, her beautiful mother Beulah, who dressed scantily and walked like a temptress. Cathy was horrified when Beulah asked her if she had a boyfriend and demonstrated how she could please him by just the move of her waist. Marg had frowned and told her mother; this is why she never brought her friends over.

Cathy on the other hand was envious of Marg having such a liberal mother. Her parents were strict and certain topics were taboo to them. Especially the sex topic since according to her mom, it was a dirty act and one not to be talked about, freely. What she knew about relationships between men and women she got from friends, tv shows and the easily available information online.

Marg became her instant friend after she was introduced to her by her grandmother. Her parents had gone to seek out greener pastures when she was three and they came back home when she turned twelve after having built three boarding houses and their main house which they still occupied till to date.

Cathy was struggling to make friends and adjust to what she considered the new atmosphere. It was after church when her mother introduced her to a kind old woman who turned out to have been Margaret's grandmother.

Margaret didn't mind at all about her accent or Englishness as some of the children had claimed in the neighborhood. She was sweet and maintained that meeting her weird family would make Cathy realize that she was unique in her own way and wasn't meant to change that.

When she finally did meet Margaret's family, she was gobsmacked. Diversity under one roof is what she termed it.

Beulah stood out from the rest, with her natural beauty and elegant grace. Her genes had definitely passed onto her daughter because Marg was an attractive lady if she tried to put her mind to it, and she glided when she walked, just like her mother.

Even if she didn't like that side about her mom, men still looked when she moved despite her young age, because the girl had learnt on how to catch male attention without trying to, no wonder Garret didn't have a chance.

They were just some women who could invoke certain images in a man's mind before they spoke their first word. Like their main purpose was to just keep a man having that wicked smile of having received a treat. She had seen that look on Garret and thought about what the Johnson old ladies said over the fence to her house when they were talking to her mother.

"He will be bringing that Jezebel into our church and this is your daughter's fault."

Cathy had snorted. "How is it my fault, I don't go to your church. Marg is my best friend and not at all what you claim she is. For God's sake, she is only eighteen years old."

"Eighteen with a lot of practice. I wonder how the Pastor's family sleeps at night knowing they would be joining their family to that polygamous lot," Grandma Freda Johnson finished then excused herself to her house. After all she didn't like to gossip, she reminded them of that.

Cathy merely rolled her eyes and never told Marg about the confrontation but she knew Margaret had a long way to go before she got accepted by some of the congregants in that church. Especially since she didn't take an active role in it. Cathy of course knew that the relationship was fake, what she had doubted was Garret not falling in love with the beauty and making it official. He had just done that.

"By the way, who is spreading the rumor that I lost it yesterday? Oh, I shouldn't have asked," Marg answered her own question when she saw her girlfriend's expression. Kells.

"Indeed, she figured the reason why Garret chose you over her cousin is because you are your mother's daughter. One dance had him singing like a canary and blinded with lust. In her eyes, your relationship is doomed."

Marg huffed then she smiled, "Let her believe that, if it makes her sleep well at night. As you know I will never do that to Garret. I want him to love me for me and not because I have made his head reel so that he can't think straight."

Cathy laughed. "Besides," Marg shrugged her shoulders, "Whoever heard of a man sticking with a woman who could be boneless while they did it. That's a mirth which my mom proved false. Dad still went for other women after her."

"Ok—ok. Are you not going to clear up the huge misunderstanding though?"

"Why should I?"

Cathy rolled her eyes, "What if the info about you doing what you aren't meant to be doing, by the way and making our poor Pastor useless goes to the wrong ears and you are forced to marry."

Marg winked

"Seriously," Cathy screeched. Marg rolled her eyes and laughed, not caring that some of the students in the canteen had looked their way.

"I want to be independent like you Cathy. That's what you used to say and now you are contemplating being stuck with him. Margaret Fletcher you are actually contemplating what your family has always wanted for you, marriage!"

"Yep girlfriend. Garret doesn't mind either. He hinted that he will eventually ask for my hand in marriage, so what's the fuss? Who says I can't have the best of both worlds too?" she said with a wink and got up while Cathy longed to hear those same words from her boyfriend.

Ralph no longer acted the same after they took their relationship to the next level. He usually said they were cool yet his actions proved that whatever had held him spellbound before, the spark, if she could call it that, was gone.

Marg wasn't aware of her lapse in judgment and the fact that she had slept with Ralph. She was too ashamed to tell her since they had both sworn to remain virgins till marriage.

Getting up and trailing behind her happy friend, for once she wished she could turn back the hands of time and like Marg not have slept with her boyfriend.

Chapter 12

"Are you serious?" Marg squealed over the phone while Garret chuckled. "What did my nana do once she met you?" she asked.

"What was she meant to do?"

She snorted and lay back on the bed. Tugging at her curls, before she looked at her fingers, she contemplated on getting a manicure. The fact that her brothers had taken Garret to meet her grandmother meant they approved of him. The family matriarch's acceptance would mean that he was a good man.

"One glance at me she couldn't help but smother me with kisses, I am a magnet when it comes to the ladies."

She laughed elated that her granny liked him. Her grandma happened to have been the first wife to her grandfather, Arnold Fletcher.

Polygamy ran in the family. While Marriam Fletcher stayed away from the drama that usually took place, her stance to the other co-wives made her seem snobbish hence, she was never liked. After a long mysterious illness which almost took her life, Marriam one day woke up a very different person. It was mysterious due to the fact that science couldn't pinpoint what ailed her, except she continued wasting away and losing her strength. She couldn't walk and she had suddenly become blind. The transformation made the other co wives claim she was a witch. Marg found out later on when she was twelve that her granny, in that moment when she felt she was dying, turned to the unseen God and cried for help. He saved her and healed her of her infirmities.

Her relationship with her Savior afterwards is what grated more on the family than anything else, hence the slander over her being evil and a witch.

"Do you know what they say about my granny?"

"Ha-ha. I did see your strong brothers' quirk in her presence. Gifford literally ran out of there when she took one glance at him and asked who he was with the previous night. The woman certainly didn't look like his fiancée. Godfrey was advised to remain faithful to his wife or else he was bound to lose her."

Marg giggled. "She sees."

"I know. A prayerful woman too."

"How did you figure it out? Mostly my family thinks she practices dark magic?"

"We got to talking and I didn't get that vibe of speaking with a different spirit."

"Ooh, how come I usually forget you are a minister?"

Garret snorted while Marg smiled. "It's because you want to continue speaking whatever pops into your mind, that's why, you conveniently forget that I'm a minister of the word."

"I miss you."

"You see," Garret said.

Now it was her turn to huff. "I miss you too sweetie," Garret said grudgingly like she had literally forced him to say so, before they went on to discuss her assignment.

She was happy at the fact that her granny approved of him. Despite how crazy her family might act, they did place the full respect over their grandmother's every word, including her father who could have that drowned puppy look every time he encountered his mother's full force.

She usually said to him, one day people will wonder what happened to the womanizer when you encounter your Savior. These women will leave you because you would have become useless.

Marg would giggle at that thought. Her father had the audacity to ask her to call one of her girlfriends, Innu so he said a few words to her, to be rendered useless where women were concerned, she couldn't wait to witness the day.

Innu was horrified of course and Marg had realized her blunder when it was already too late and her dad was handing Innu the wad of cash. He had tricked her by saying Innu was a new friend. He knew Cathy and Gina but hadn't met Innu. The sweet girl almost passed out and was furious with her for a week.

After they made up and joked over the matter, Marg had advised. You should have taken the money and bought yourself something with it. Serves him right for not giving any to his daughter.

She was horrified when shame-faced Innu confessed that she did take it and gave him a fake phone number, while Marg jokingly called her step mom.

The girls ate out for a while, courtesy of Innu and bought a couple of outfits to wear when they went out clubbing. Marg knew that her family was certainly the bane of her life.

"Can't wait for the exam month to end so I see you again." She commented over the phone, after they had finished with her assignment. More like her boyfriend had been pointing out the different conditions she had spelt under one branch, evil spirit or demon, including pulling up a couple of verses to that effect. His life was way easier than hers at the moment, she thought.

"Same here sweets."

"Can't you pay me a visit? A tiny little visit. Pretty please my dear princeling." Marg excitedly asked. Why hadn't she thought of that in the first place.

Garret chuckled before he answered, "Nope."

Her mouth gaped open at the finality in his voice before she snapped it shut and snorted.

"Why not?"

"Your granny advised me to stay away from you. She said "you will jump my bones.""

She coughed, spluttered, wheezed, rose from her sleeping position while she clutched at the phone, and tears ran down her face from the coughing fit.

"Are you okay baby," Garret's concerned voice drifted through. After clearing her throat, she muttered, "I will survive," before she screeched, "You can't be serious!"

Her boyfriend had the nerve to laugh. "I am serious. Your grandmother, the prophetess by the way if you have conveniently forgotten, said it. Not me. When she eventually gives the go ahead, I will get onto that plane and be there in no time at all."

Marg huffed. Why did everyone think all of a sudden, she would drag him to bed? This was all Kells and her snooty cousin Simone's fault. Their little mudslinging must have gotten to the parents too.

"Any plans for your birthday next month," Garret asked her. Marg grinned widely as she could hear the smile in his voice. What was her hunk, up to?

"That's covered, my brothers usually hold a bash for me, did you have anything in mind like proposing to me." Garret laughed, "You see why your granny said that statement. You are too eager. What happened to your independence?"

"I fell in love with a juicy morsel of flesh," Marg said and heard Garret grumble. "I do hope Greg makes the right choice of a woman in future, because having a person like you is completely embarrassing."

She snorted and hung up on him. He called a few seconds later, placated her as he usually did and they went on to talk sweet nothings till she fell asleep.

Chapter 13

Seriously! Margaret tightly wrapped her red silk robe around her, after having taken a long, relaxing bath and smearing the heavenly smelling body lotion over her body. For a middle-class girl, she was likely to grow and strut feathers like a peacock after this treatment.

Garret had sent the early birthday gift along with the car that picked her up with Cathy at the airport.

Seriously! Her mind screamed again for the second time.

The soothing bath might have done wonders to her body, but she was still irritated to the brim as she tried to untangle the confusion in her mind.

Here she was stuck in her room after her family members failed to wish her a happy birthday. Was it because she hadn't lived up to their expectations of her, the reason why they were being this cold. The twins didn't throw the usual bash and her friends too appeared to not have bothered texting or taking her out.

The world was surely an unsympathetic place. Only one person had thought about her from the time she left school, her boyfriend.

Garret bought two first class plane tickets, for her and Cathy. While Marg was now used to traveling in that manner after she became Garret's fake girlfriend, once they got to the airport, Cathy had squealed in delight when they made use of the VIP terminal before they plopped down in the comfy first-class seats, very much different to the economy class they were used to.

Marg humored Cathy by getting excited too; they had giggled and chatted like the teens they were. That was before Cathy uttered those dastard words, managing to make Marg's world tilt on its axis.

I envy you. I wish I could go back in time and treat Ralph differently. Maybe he would look at me the way Garret still does to you. With love and admiration, like you are the most precious thing that has ever happened to him.

Marg had stared at Cathy in confusion before her friend gathered up the courage to tell her about her slip up with Ralph. Apparently, sex had destroyed them somehow, since Ralph wasn't the same person she knew, who was always quick to put her first.

What a shocker, of all things Marg never imagined a time when Cathy would one day throw caution to the winds and let loose.

For goodness' sake, Cathy was brought up well and had a strong religious footing, unlike her who happened to be a rolling stone. Everyone assumed that she had ventured into the deep waters, even though she was dating a pastor, while her saintly friend waited for marriage.

With the way she and Garret would get all passionate at times, it was a surprise they hadn't torn each other's clothes off their backs, in the few moments they met after being an official couple.

She now realized why her mother would insist she got married to Garret, the soonest. Both her parents' genes in her were a total disaster. She craved for Garret's touch like fish craved for water. Her saving grace was that she was in another city, at school and Garret was usually busy with the church, hence his mind didn't zone out and move to unchartered waters like hers was prone to.

Having tried meditating and instantly given up the moment those little birdies in her head changed and became Garret, with a partially open shirt and winked at her, Marg tried being still and doing breathing exercises that were likely to calm her nerves.

That went pretty well, because a beautiful picture of her handsome hunk flipped in her mind again and this time, he was lifting weights. Sweat glimmered on his well-toned body, that had her heart speeding up and her hands furiously flapping over her heated face.

Then she thought, why not starve the body of food. Who knew that senses overcompensated, she thought in dismay? She then consulted her minister boyfriend, pretending the cousin of someone she knew was going through the burning phase.

A simple answer from her man, self-denial and severe bodily discipline can't help a person in conquering one's evil desires.

The coughing started like the one after her granny's statement.

He should have said that earlier and she wouldn't have gone without food for a freaking whole day.

Evil, what was this thing about evil desires?

Bottom line, she threw in the towel, her attempts futile and resigned to the thought that her boyfriend would be strong for the both of them.

When Cathy said her bit about her one time slip up, Marg was quick to encourage her friend to be the strong one, seeing Ralph wouldn't be that for the both of them and made her swear, to Cathy's chagrin, that she would in no way open those legs again for Ralph until he married her.

Margaret drooped her shoulders in dismay and walked back into her room, that was a tall order and she knew it, considering she battled with her hormones too.

The last time she and Garret were together, oh my—not that she would mention that to Cathy. She knew if she hadn't fought with Garret, the day he came over to visit, she, like her best friend, would be in the same boat now.

They had been making out in his hotel room, when he removed the shirt and she finally saw the beautiful tattoo in all its glory. One question is all it took, to sap the intimate atmosphere from exhilarating to the cold, unyielding one that soon followed, since Garret pulled away after that.

"What was happening in your life, the time you had this done?"

She was stroking his strong arm when Garret, instead of continuing kissing her like he had been doing on her neck, abruptly stood up from the bed like she had scalded him with hot water.

His eyes narrowed and for a second, a look of distrust overshadowed them, while she felt a cold tingling sensation pass down her spine.

Not again, she thought, and pressed further with her guard now up too. "It can't be that terrible for you to shut me out like this," she softly said.

Garret reached out to the shirt that had been carelessly flung in the heat of the moment and donned it on. The more those buttons covered his beautiful, muscled and well-toned body, the more his face appeared to be shutting down too.

Shutters hiding more than opening to reveal his past. He literally commanded her to make herself presentable, instead of being the temptation she was, after he was done with making himself presentable. Marg hadn't moved an inch from where he had left her.

She rolled her eyes, very much familiar with that evasive tactic and she wasn't going to let him shut down like before.

Last time on Christmas he had that luxury since they were pretending to be dating then. Pulling back her short doll dress that had been riding on her hips, she clasped her bra back into place and adjusted her dress straps.

She asked again, narrowed her eyes too, having forgotten that a while ago, his kisses had almost made her forget her name.

"Babe," Garret motioned with his hand. "Just take it as one of those silly things I did in my early teens and leave it at that. This is me now. I don't get it why you have to bring this up all the time. I would rather have my girlfriend with me, right here at this moment than a shrink analyzing my past."

She bristled. Of all things, how could he say that? And to think she had told him everything about herself, including her silly childhood mistakes while he gave nothing of himself. To be fair he had talked about his happy childhood, but she still couldn't wrap the other part over her head that she was Garret's first girlfriend.

He was freaking handsome, successful, monied and in no way was it possible that he hadn't broken a few hearts in the process before they met.

Then there was the damning evidence of how he would touch her, make her body tingle, sing and lose control, she knew, she just felt it, that he was more experienced than he was letting on. While her body would take over her senses, his body had a restraint about it that could only be pulled off by a man of experience. Her mom had mentioned that once men ceased to think with their heads, it was always game on. Apparently, her man could be excluded from that brand, because Garret was always in control, no matter what.

She walked to where he stood and hugged him from the back.

"Do you know that secrets have a way of coming out and the character of a person eventually gets revealed. Bad boys are always bad boys, no matter how hard they try to hide it."

The statement was made partly as a joke, to dispel the atmosphere that had suddenly settled in the room.

She wasn't looking for a fight, but apparently her man didn't see it that way and left her splattering and fumbling for words to take back what she had said. Stiffening and becoming unresponsive to the hug, he ground out, "If I am bad, then why do you hang out with me, Margaret Fletcher?" before he walked out of the room, leaving her standing in a daze.

And to think Cathy envied her relationship with Garret! Wow. Ralph was an open book where she was concerned. At least Ralph had been honest with Cathy that he had his fair share of women before he met her.

Marg wondered how she could still desire the person who was so evasive about his past.

Abruptly coming to a halt in her room, her mouth hung open as the man who always featured in every one of her fantasies stood, leaning near her study table and grinned. Rubbing her eyes, the ever-present butterflies quivered in her tummy while she took in his dark tailored suit and attractive grin.

Hell, this wasn't a day dream, it was real. He was right there in her room!

"Happy birthday baby," Garret said, walked over to where she stood, still stuck to the floor and hugged her. She inhaled the familiar musky scent and sighed before he tilted her chin and kissed her.

She forgot all her misgivings she had been having a while back, when Garett touched her and instead, enjoyed the delicious kiss which was better than her dreams as it managed to make all the sensitive parts in her body heat up and quiver. Wrapping her arms around his neck, and moaning in delight, his hands were splayed at her back before they lowered, squeezed her bottom as she drew closer to him.

Marg giggled as her hulk swiftly picked her up and she straddled him before she continued relishing the deep passionate kisses, he delivered with finesse belying the title of junior pastor without any carnal experience.

His hard body so intimately pressed against her soft one, his scent, his heat, proved heady to her already reeling senses as she couldn't get enough of him and wanted more. She had tugged the shirt from his slacks, naughtily skimmed his strong body with her nails and delighted over how silky soft and warm his skin felt. Just one slight movement and she will be opening up those buttons to get a better view.

How she loved him and the thought of losing him hurt like hell. What if his past would tear them apart and hence, he was protecting her from it? He was here with her right at this moment, wasn't he? She slightly pulled away and mouthed, love me, before she kissed him again as his hands ran possessively over her body.

Garret literally wrenched his mouth from her and for a second looked dazed while she tried to catch her breath. He slid her body back on the floor.

This is a mistake; Marg shamefully thought and lowered her eyes.

"Marg," he whispered, and she briefly shut her eyes, not wanting to see the accusation in them over her wanton behavior.

He cupped her face. "Open your eyes honey," he softly said as she slowly opened them. No judgment but love piercing through them.

"I love you," he said. Marg smiled. He opened his mouth to speak further except they were interrupted by her mom's yelling.

"Are you giving Marg the gift you bought for her, or your visit has turned into something else?"

Garret laughed and shifted before he reached out to the box on her study table.

"In case you think your family has abandoned you on your birthday. For this time, I asked them to not have the party because I wanted to spend this day with you."

Marg opened her mouth to retort, since she had already been fuming over that fact.

"Pastor Gee, your ten minutes is up, I'm coming up there," her mother yelled.

Garret chuckled, swiftly kissed her and walked out of the room

"Be down in 5 minutes or I am gone," he ordered by the door, while she huffed and opened the box.

She gasped at seeing the outfit. Her eyes widened at the tag. Ethan made this. Unbelievable, she thought then giggled and got ready for her date with her man.

Chapter 14

"We are here love." Marg looked outside and only saw a dark filled night.

"Here, where?"

"Our destination of course."

No way, this couldn't be what Garret had planned. So, to get this straight, she had missed out on the huge bash that her brothers always organized for her, for this!

Her eyes widened on her boyfriend while he chuckled at her expense.

"I don't see any buildings here."

"They are there Marg, relax, it's not the middle of nowhere, even if it was, don't you trust me?"

Ha, ha, joke on me, she thought as her hands became clammy with sweat. Despite their values, Garret was a man after all and she was a woman who had been playing with fire.

Could she trust him? For some reason she had always thought him safe, even an hour or so ago in her room, he had remained the perfect gentleman after she had literally begged him to make love to her.

She furiously fanned her face, as the butterflies in her tummy started again. Was this pay back for her wanton ways?

"Marg." He was staring at her. She gulped a few breaths of air and produced a wobbly smile. "Have you ever heard of dark themed restaurants where night vision goggles are only worn by the staff in attendance."

"I might have, is this place like that?"

Garret nodded

"Why of all things would you consider that as a good birthday gift for me?"

He shrugged his shoulders. "I thought nineteen-year-old Margie baby was in the mood to try out new things." He opened the door and came out of the car, while she bit hard on her lip.

Nineteen-year-old Marg had thought she was ready for adult stuff, but as it turned out, she was a chicken.

Finally, she came out of the car. Garret took her hand and started leading her to only the Lord knew where.

"I wonder why my trying out new things had to be this?" Marg nervously giggled, trying to stem the flow of her wild thoughts. She looked around, not able to identify much. It was dark so as to be expected, her eyes always acted up in the dark. While others could easily point out the outlines and shape of things, her vision usually decided to go on sleep mode.

"Augh," she groaned and clutched at Garrets arm while he led her to the building. Be extreme Marg, she thought and said, "This is so frustrating, I mean who needs a blindfold when they are blind as a bat. Does that saying make any sense to you."

Garret chuckled. She could feel the rumble of his laughter and she smirked. "Wait a minute, did you bring me out here to have your wicked way with me. Finish what we started in my room." They were now standing still, so when he spoke loudly and said, "Margaret Fletcher," his voice having the dismayed note, she giggled. "Relax honey, don't act like you haven't been thinking about it."

Garret growled and spoke loudly again, "please let's get this over with before she says something even worse and my face gets beaten to a pulp."

Before Marg could ask on who he was talking to, the lights came on while people hollered, Surprise!! Happy birthday!!

Her mom, dad, step brothers, the doctors looking at all unimpressed, step mothers, his parents, brother, friends, she couldn't look any further since her eyes had become tiny slits as it dawned that she had been saying all those things in front of them.

She looked at Garret who was shaking his head with a smile on his face. "Gosh you are so embarrassing," he whispered, while Marg looked in horror at his grandmother who was clutching at her sides and laughing. "How do I explain to everyone that our conduct has been above board? See you brothers look like they are about to tie my balls into knots," Garret asked.

His mom heard him and pulled Marg who seemed mortified into her arms. "Don't worry about that dear, happy birthday Marg, son, lay off the vulgar language please."

"Thank you, Mrs. Henderson. You hear that, at least here is someone who understands me in that I was just pulling your leg."

Garret shook his head and left her with his mother while he walked over to his little brother and her brothers.

"Come on, Garret's Nana needs to meet you," his mother said with a smile.

Marg lowered her eyes as they walked to her grandmother and his.

"Marjorie my girl, happy birthday." Her granny said and hugged her.

"Granny, I am not Marjorie...", she didn't continue since her granny seemed to be beaming like she had always known that this was her granddaughter and not daughter.

"Let me look at you." Evelyn, Garret's granny said. Marg was engulfed in a hug before Eve looked her over. "Mhm." She nodded her head in approval. "Garret made a good choice. Remember you first child belongs to me seeing you already have a head start," she joked, while Marg blushed and prayed Garret would come to her rescue. He was right that no one would believe their relationship to be innocent after her big mouth said those words.

At least Cathy could be comforted too in knowing that she wasn't the only one struggling with her flesh. She glanced at her friend who had come with her boyfriend. Ralph leaned in to say something to her. Cathy vehemently shook her head while Marg wondered if he had called her out for a quickie, seeing he walked away sulking and Cathy stared at her before she winked. Marg giggled.

"A dance with the birthday girl," Garret asked her then winked at her. Marg accepted his hand after excusing herself from their grandparents and walked to the middle of the room.

Marg inhaled sharply when Garret wrapped his hand on her waist and pulled her close as slow music played in the background. As to be expected, it was one of her brothers' latest love songs, very clean and different from their other crude songs.

"Are you not afraid that I might do something more to embarrass you?"

Garret laughed, "Nah, you wouldn't dare with all these people around. I'm safe."

She huffed, twirled in his arms before their dance slowed further and she could feel his breath on her neck, raising the small hairs on her nape.

"We really need to discuss your forwardness."

Marg profusely blushed and lowered her eyes. His hand splayed possessively on the small of her back, drew her closer still, hitching her breath even more before he leaned in and whispered in a growl, close to her ear. "Are you really nineteen and a virgin?" Marg shivered then pouted her cute lips before she guiltily looked away from him.

Garret must have sensed what she was thinking because he slightly frowned before he hugged her and kissed her on the forehead.

"Never think what you feel is wrong Marg. At least we both definitely know that we look forward to being intimate with each other and we will both enjoy the copulation when we get married."

Marg pinched him and giggled, "Garret baby, be careful of what you wish for." Her eyes widened in wonder at what he had said too. "Married," she softly spoke.

Garret watched her cute full lips with that seductive smile of a temptress while her eyes literally sparkled.

The ladies who had been witness to the Fletchers must have felt the same spell, he thought.

Instead of thinking her forward and not wanting to see a smidgen of shame like he had glimpsed a while back and also in her room, like it was wrong for her to feel that way and show him that she desired him, he decided to act, Marg belonged by his side forever.

He loved her and all of her, with that uncontrollable passion that was tottering at the edge. She was literally quivering in his arms.

Looking at Gifford the crazy twin, he nearly laughed when the twin pointed between his eyes with two fingers, double tapped and pointed his way, to signal that he was watching him.

It was now or never, Garett thought before he stopped dancing, or it was their swaying since their dance was no longer that at all, but two bodies slightly swaying as one.

Marg curiously looked at his face. Clearing up his throat he knelt down with his eyes on her.

He could hear his mom gasp, while her mom sniffled and received a hanky from the father. Drama queens, he thought, since they had been on his case on what the delay was. They didn't buy it at all that he would wait for Marg till she finished school. That's when her mother had also added her advice, my Margie girl is a lot like me. It's a matter of time before she gets you into her bed. We wouldn't want that for our junior pastor right. Brought low by a slip of a woman all because he would prefer to wait till she finished her studies. Thanks a lot for the nudge soon to be mother-in-law.

Marg had already clasped her hand over her mouth in shock.

"Yes married...Margaret Fletcher, love of my life, please do me the honors of becoming my wife. I love you...I don't have the flowery words to say what you might want to hear,"

She chuckled. One thing I do promise you is that I will love and cherish you for the rest of my life. Will you sweet Marg, marry me.

Marg vigorously nodded her head and he chuckled before he slid the ring on her finger and stood up. Some shouts and ululations could be heard while the family drifted to them and congratulated them.

He had already asked for permission from her dad a few days before she came back home for the holidays, hence the man winked when he saw his daughter scream to her friend, Cathy who had attended the party with Ralph, Lily boy and his girlfriend and Gina before she hugged them. A quick glance to the door had him narrowing his eyes at the thought of a matter he still had to handle before he and Marg lived happily ever after.

He found him in the well-lit and still empty barn. He was yet to tell Marg that this would be their home.

"Bill," he said as Bill lounged on one of the wooden steps with a bottle in hand.

"Garret Henderson, it's been long." Bill said before he looked at him.

Why had he never realized the resemblance with Marg even if it was slight. When she mentioned him that's when it had dawned on him and he has always known he will come across him. Seven years couldn't erase the memories he still had. The past that he couldn't deny, at the same time the past he couldn't go back to.

"Does she know what you are?" was the question he asked after gulping in more of the alcohol.

Garret clenched his hands on the side and as he was prone to, to hide what he really felt and gave him a cold stare.

"People change," he answered.

Her brother stood up and slightly swayed before he took another swig from the bottle.

"Can a leopard really change its spots? That's a new one."

A pause while Garret watched him through narrowed eyes.

"That's my little sis dammit, what kind of life will you give her."

"I will make her happy."

Bill glared at him. "Very typical of a Henderson to think that by the flick of your finger, all will be cleared off just like that."

"What happened in the past Bill, what I believed then, is very much different from what I believe now and who I am. I was young and confused. You very much know that."

"What are you saying?"

Garret pointed at his own chest and answered, "I am not that."

For a second, Bill appeared to be staggered by what he had said before he furiously walked towards him.

"Say it Garret, you are not what? Why are you afraid of voicing it out? Just like you were afraid then in admitting it, you still are doing the same till to date. There is no need to feel guilty about it no matter what your father says."

When he got to the last step, Bill stumbled and by reflex, Garret caught him.

Bill snaked his hand over his neck and said near his ear, "I still love you; I will wait for you to come to your senses and admit the truth that you and your bloody family have kept hidden all this while."

A gasp was heard coming from the door, Marg with wide open eyes as she clutched at her throat in shock.

Bill merely ran his eyes over her and stated, "let me leave you two to talk, no need to rush away Maggie." He sneered and walked past her before Marg nervously wiped at the sweat that had gathered on her brow.

Did she just dream up everything? Her nerves were frayed as it was. She had looked around to catch a glimpse of her fiancé to no avail, after showing off the ring to her friends and chatting with her mom. That was until Cliff pointed to the door.

Her mom couldn't keep the secret any longer. She had whispered to her that this building she actually was having her party at, was the farmhouse Garret had built for his family.

"My Margie baby will be having her own place, can't wait to visit you when you tie the knot and look in on my grandchildren."

Marg had giggled and taken in everything. With the lights on, she realized, this is what she would have imagined for herself too. The farmhouse was beautiful, especially the huge hall where the party was being hosted. She could just imagine holding such parties in future with both of their huge families not cramping the space at all. She couldn't wait to inspect the kitchen and bedrooms except Garret wasn't at her side to do so.

Reaching the barn, she was shaken up by Bill leaning over him before he said, in a voice that she could clearly hear. I still love you.

She was surprised when her voice came out clearly, without the fear that was suddenly gnawing at her, thinking of when she spoke about Bill and how Garret's mood suddenly changed.

Garret had still not turned to face her. She licked her suddenly dry lips. "You are...," she didn't finish because he whirled to face her and glared at her. "I know what you are about to say, don't even say it because it's not true."

Stupid, stupid, stupid. Why hadn't she read the signs? The coldness at the mention of her brother, the affectionate way he treated Ethan Ross.

Garret might have thought she never noticed how differently he treated that young man from the rest of Greg's friends.

She thought back to Christmas, this time with clear perceptive eyes as every misgiving she ever held, finally fell into place. While Garret had stood aloof and she turned to listen to Dominic, Ethan had walked up to Garret and they left together.

They came back an hour or so, citing they had been playing basketball. Ethan had winked at him, before he had added casually, as usual, your boyfriend won.

Could they have, she savagely wiped her lips at the thought of his lips that had kissed her with so much passion and suddenly felt sick in her gut.

"You are," Marg trudged on, despite the warning in his eyes. Garret began to walk towards her.

"Marg," a growl could be heard in his voice. Marg shifted, stepping back slowly till the back of her legs hit the wall to the barn.

"You are gay," she accusingly stated, saying aloud the loathed words she had been failing to summon after the shock hit her.

Garett growled menacingly before reaching where she stood, backed into the wall with no way of escape. He was close enough that she could feel the heat emanate from his body and sniff at the cologne she so loved. Close enough to make her want to fling her arms over his neck and see the eyes smolder with passion and desire for her, except this time a coldness lay in their depth.

Close enough to long to go back in time before her beautiful life was shuttered by the realization of this betrayal. Secrets always managed to come into light.

"Marg, you do not know what you are talking about. I am not." Garret clamped his jaw and Marg could clearly see how hard he was trying to hold back whatever emotion he might have felt at her announcement.

"I saw you with my brother and I heard what he said."

He crossed his arms, shutting himself further away from her with that cold look that he could pull out so well.

Garret wasn't denying it, she thought. She looked at his stance, all male testosterone from head to toe, not like her brother Bill and Greg's friend Ethan.

Narrowing her eyes to tiny slits, she watched him too, cold and aloof. Too many years of being overlooked had taught her that. She might have been naive to things that concerned relationships, hers with Garret being the first relationship she ever got into, but that didn't mean the books her mom had sometimes accused her of being in, didn't give her all the information she needed to know, or her friends. She knew when two people had the hots for each other and no rocket science was required there.

"I never thought I would see this day. All the time I had been barking up the wrong tree thinking you will one day leave me for another woman and never realizing that you might be attracted not to the opposite but to your—."

"Marg!" Garret bellowed and made her flinch as it dawned that she had taken it too far. Would he want to prove her wrong? Fear and dread filled her up because if he touched her, she knew she wouldn't resist him, despite knowing he didn't love her but had used her.

Bill had done the same too, hiding his secret until his mom found out that the person, he used to call Jossey, was actually a man, Josiah.

Their father couldn't accept that about his son, having figured it out hence disinherited him instantly.

Bill is the only one who used his mother's maiden name. His relationship with his father after the discovery made it more tumultuous as compared to before. Arnold Fletcher couldn't look at him and not think himself a failure for having one who perverted the very foundations of what a man is. He had given Bill an ultimatum once he turned twenty-one, settle down with a good woman or forever be an outcast in his eyes. No matter what his wives and Bill's mother might have said in that they love their children unconditionally, that seemed to fall on deaf ears because Fletcher was willing to lose his son.

Could Garret, unlike Bill, have chosen to pretend, knowing his family was strong in their religious views. She believed apart from being together, they had been friends too, so why didn't he tell her. Garett sighed and ran his finger over her face before he leaned in and kissed her. What she had feared rearing to the forefront as she responded the same way she always had. Her body slightly swayed as she was filled with disgust on how she would want him.

The kiss went on and on before they resurfaced back and drew in their breath. Slightly shifting and not at all shocked by her reaction, Marg held up her hands and with a plea in her eyes, looked at the man she loved, as her heart broke into a million pieces.

"Please be honest with me and yourself just this once. Where you in love with Bill and in a relationship with him. Is this why you couldn't talk about your past?"

She held her breath. Garret shifted away from her and drooped his shoulders before he nodded.

A sob escaped her lips before she wrenched the engagement ring from her finger and tossed it at him.

For a while she had thought she would be able to handle the truth. Now when he didn't deny her worst fears, fury did rise for the fool he had turned her into.

"To hell with you Garret Henderson and your lies. What is this, was I just a pawn. An experiment to you, being the first woman you have actually been with."

Garret pityingly looked at her and opened his mouth. That was worse, she looked away and rushed out of the barn.

Garret grimaced, crouched and retrieved the ring that had been furiously flung at him.

He pinched the bridge of his nose, an indicator of the tension he felt.

"I am sorry Marg," he whispered before he stood up from his crouching position and walked to the car.

That precious, beautiful girl he loved with his whole heart deserved more than he could ever give her. A man without his past.

Chapter 15

"Sweet heart, what is going on," Garret's mother asked when she got into his office at church. It was the next day in the morning, different by all means as to how he had felt the day before in anticipation of the surprise party he intended to host for his girlfriend.

"Nothing ma."

She scoffed and narrowed her eyes. "Yesterday Marg said she suddenly had a terrible headache and excused herself from the rest, while you were nowhere to be found. Today when I went over to get her so we went out shopping, she said the wedding was off and I should ask you. Did you have a lover's tiff of some sort?"

"We both realized we were not good for each other."

His mom stood akimbo and narrowed her eyes further. "When did that new development happen seeing you gathered both families for the huge proposal to the love of your life."

"You should be relieved ma, that Fletcher will no longer be your in law."

His mother huffed. "Since when does any member of this family care about one's reputation." She shifted and sat back on the chair opposite him.

"Honey, tell me the honest truth. What really happened last night, and please don't give me those lame excuses, you have never been good at lying."

Garret placed his pen on the sheets of papers he had been going through, before his mother came into his office.

"Yesterday, Margaret found out about my past."

"What do you mean she found out yesterday. Did you not tell her before you started dating?"

Garret grimaced. Of course, he had tried to tell her. The first time was when he dropped her off at school. Before he could utter the words, her friends dragged her off away from him. On Vee Day, he got furious over a man on her side and ended up kissing her senselessly to mark his territory. Yesterday she had looked so happy and content, hence he had produced the ring instead.

"Did you not explain to her that you are not gay?"

"I did and she is not buying it."

"I will go and explain it to her then, Marg is a reasonable girl."

"No ma, don't." He shook his head while his mom frowned at him.

"Garret, whatever happened to you wasn't your fault. What that m—man," her voice faltered, "did to you wasn't your choice, no matter how he justified everything."

"I know ma, but that boat sailed long back don't you think. Of accusing someone else for my actions. Despite seeing the pain, this all caused to the family and to me, for a while after in my teens I did believe that lie and had male relations."

She shut her ears in dismay. Garret stood up from his chair and walked up to her before he removed her hands from her ears.

"I am not perfect, ma. God healed and delivered me from the bondage of that sin, but not all people can believe that. With our confused world, it is so easy to believe that our vices can never be removed. That desire for men is totally gone and I desire women. Hell, I desire Marg with my whole being."

His mother chuckled and told him not to swear.

He grinned and she touched his face. "Why are you not saying these same words to her?"

Garret shrugged.

"Don't tell me it's about Ru again. Marg is a sensible girl, different from her, above everything she loves you son. I have seen it in every way. She has even brought you out of that imposed exile. You are good together. You talk more, relate more with other people, can't you see that?"

Garret was silent while he looked at his mother's pleading eyes.

What she was saying, he knew already. He might enjoy the company of the youths, but never could he claim to be friends with them. They always looked up to him as their pastor, while Marg on the other hand and her crew of friends, made him feel comfortable and he had been able to just be himself.

His mother sighed. "With Greg I know when he feels misunderstood, he acts impulsively to fix the misunderstanding. I wish at times you would be like him. You my son, close up. You hide behind that cold stare and little do people actually realize that it's a defense mechanism to hide your insecurity. Fine, I will not talk about marriage seeing you have made up your mind. Although I would have loved it if Marg were to be my daughter in law." She finished wistfully, kissed him on his forehead before she stood from her chair and walked out.

"See you in the evening," she whispered, then shut the door behind her.

Garret sat on the chair she had vacated. For one thing his mother was right, he also would have wanted Marg to be his wife. He cradled his head and said a silent prayer.

"Margie baby, are you going to stay up in bed for the whole day," her mother asked and got into her room. She felt terrible. Her eyes were puffy from the crying she had been doing after she ran out on Garret. How could he have been so cruel and made her believe that good men were out there and he was one of them?

His mother had checked up on her, so they could do their shopping but she refused even to see her. Lucille, as to be expected, was stubborn and finally she summoned the courage to meet with her and tell her the wedding was off. She had been shocked.

Her mother opened the blinds in her room and settled down next to her before she retrieved the tray she had brought along with her from the dresser.

"Sit up love, you should eat something."

Marg shook her head and mumbled, "not hungry."

A palm of her cool mother's hand could be felt on her forehead before she asked softly, "Are you pregnant?"

Marg abruptly sat up.

"Ma!" She yelled.

"What, I know you kids nowadays, you can't wait to experience that side of love. I have seen those looks shared between you and my son in law. You tear each other's clothes off your bodies by just the stares. Then the dance yesterday, Mmhm, said it all."

Thanks, ma, for the visuals that are always handy, Marg almost retorted but huffed instead and said "sorry to disappoint, I am not pregnant and I will not be any time soon. I and Garret are over."

"What did you do?"

Marg groaned; it was so like her mother to assume that she was at fault. "That man who was about to be your son in law, is not what he pretends to be. Garret was once involved with Bill."

"So."

Her eyes widened. "What do you mean when you say, so?"

"I mean it was long back and people do change."

Marg couldn't believe what she was hearing. She glared at her mother who skillfully spooned the cereal and placed it near her mouth while Marg felt forced to eat it, since the spoon was literally on her mouth.

"I remember Lucille called me when she caught Bill with Garret. He was just fourteen while our Bill was eighteen. She was agitated. I knew about Bill but it seemed they weren't aware about their son being involved with him." She shook her head and spooned out more cereal for Marg to eat. "Bill had saved my number as mom, so when they called me, they assumed that I was his biological mother. Both Bill and Garret seemed shaken once I got there. I will never forget the lost look on Garret. Cornered more like it. While people accepted that their children were born that way, his father believed otherwise, that he was acting out because of an early traumatic experience. He was breathing fire and didn't care about the backlash to follow if he reported those two, as long as he got his son back. The one he knew was still there, despite his actions. Lucille and I managed to convince him to not be in a rush, hence Bill was told to stay away."

"Knowing that." Marg ate more cereal before she continued, "you still allowed your only daughter to be involved with him."

Her mother shrugged. "Honey, no one is perfect. That has been proven over and over again, by me, your father and everyone else. We each have our own share of problems that need to be brought before our Maker so we are made whole again."

"When did you start believing?" Marg asked in disbelief.

Her mother dismissively shrugged her shoulders. "It's not a matter of when I started believing, but more on when you got to be, so full of unbelief."

Marg lowered her eyes, she knew what her mom meant. After the struggle to conceive, when her mother finally did, Marg had a lot of health issues when she came into the world. She was a weak child and not one who would have survived for long.

Prayers from her grandmother kept her alive. At thirteen years old, when she went with Cathy to her church for the first time and believed in the one who was always working in the background when her grandmother prayed, the Lord Jesus, every condition she still had, miraculously vanished.

Medically speaking it was impossible, but here she was, a miracle walking. If that same God could do the impossible on her, He surely would do the same to Garret.

Gosh this was a mess. She thought of the glare she got from Garret the day before while he had warned her not to say the dreadful words. Garret desired her, that much she knew. But why hadn't he trusted her with his past. What future would they have if they didn't have that.

"When I met Mrs. Henderson a year ago and she told me about her son's transformation I believed it," her mother continued. "I caught a glimpse of Garret too and Margie baby, he was very much different from the lost boy I had seen a few years back. Was it wrong for me to agree to the set up when Marjorie suggested that you and Garret should go on a blind date despite knowing the truth." She sadly shrugged her shoulders. "I know you think your father is not a good man but you should understand that I chose to be with him and I am content. Your dad gave me a home and security, something that I never had in the streets. I wish I had been a better role model to you and when I saw Garret, for some reason I thought not only him but his family would give you what we as your parents failed to give you, since we are too broken."

She placed the spoon with satisfaction on the plate.

"You are not broken ma," Marg said and sniffled. Her mom moved from where she had been seated and hugged her.

"Just give it a long proper thought before you decide to end this for good. Garret would make a good husband because he has experienced the hand of God over his life, just like you my baby girl. You all understand that it's not about your faults but how both of you are willing to make this thing work, with God on your side. The people who have lived happy lives Marg, aren't those who strive with their own effort to make it work, they are those who realize that in and of themselves they do not have the strength but rely on one who gives them the strength. Enough," she pulled away and stood up, "I think I have spoken enough for today, my mouth aches." She stretched her lips with her hands while Marg looked at the woman, she had always considered clueless like she was seeing her for the first time. Throughout she had thought she didn't believe. Her mother didn't go to church or speak pertaining to faith, that was until this moment of course.

"Give it a thought," she said by the door. "Perfection, you will not find it anyway. If it's possible for you to get healed of every condition you ever had, it is possible for Garret to have a transformed sexuality and be what God designed him to be, not the lies the enemy might have told him whilst he was growing up."

Marg slumped on the bed and groaned. This was too much even for her.

Chapter 16

3 months later.

"Will you be okay," Cathy asked Marg, concern evident in the tone of her voice and on her face. Marg braved a smile and nodded before she firmly shut the door to her room and sat down on the floor to weep.

Her mother had called her whilst she was coming from her last lecture for the day and informed her that Garret would be marrying Simone.

How could the news hurt so much when she hadn't laid eyes on Garret ever since her birthday.

Despite her mom's word, she didn't reconcile with him and Garret never reached out to her.

He did continue sponsoring her, as the week before she was meant to travel to school, she received an air ticket from him and proof of payment for her accommodation and tuition.

Her mother advised her not to drop out but continue with what she had started.

Wailing aloud for her lost love and clutching at her heart, Marg finally dragged herself to the bathroom, when she felt she had shed all the tears that she needed to.

Gosh it really hurt, especially coming to the knowledge that Garret had quickly moved on without her.

What did her mother say? Garret and Simone were perfect for each other. Simone was ready to settle down, she was a member of his church and would likely not face any resistance like Marg would have, if their relationship had continued.

To add salt to injury, her mom was quick in pointing out, happily to the grating of her nerves, that everything had worked out for good since Marg no longer had family members insisting she got married, but was on her way to attaining her independence as she has always wanted to.

When all was said and done, Marg did indeed get her way at the end.

Was that meant to comfort her in any way? Knowing that her parents had been well meaning too when they wanted her to get married. Garret had opened this other door in her life that couldn't be shut. Of feeling loved and for once she had experienced the freedom brought about by her voice being heard.

Splashing cool water on her face, she looked at herself in the mirror and grimaced.

A week ago, she had an unexpected visitor.

Before she could angrily walk away once she realized who had called her to the parking lot, his first words stopped her in mid step. "I'm sorry little sis."

She furiously turned to face him and yelled, "Sorry for what?" After he took away her fairytale, he had the audacity to look like the hurt one in all this. Bill walked up to her. Stretched out his arms and let them fall on his side while Marg tried to remain, passive and unaffected.

"Marg, I don't know what got to me the day of your engagement."

This is useless, she thought and turned to walk away. Even the love for her step brother couldn't take away the hurt that she still felt.

"Marg, Garret never accepted that he was gay, even to date he doesn't." Bill said loudly and she whirled around to face him. Bill walked up to her and nodded, while Marg thought about the night of her birthday.

He whispered once he was close to her, "Garret used to voice out his regrets. He always felt guilty after we were together. Claimed that it was unholy." Bill chuckled. "For some reason his words never hurt me. I figured he was in denial and he was trying by all means to fight being attracted to his own kind. The day his dad caught us, that's when everything dawned on who I had actually been hanging out with and why he would use words such as unholy to describe our relationship. He was the first-born son of Graham Henderson, a minister, meaning in future that same torch would be passed onto him."

"He was a minor Bill." Instead of getting offended at the fact that Marg was blaming all this on him, Bill smiled. He met Garret a few days after he had turned eighteen, in an underground gay club. Their nation was still one of those that considered such relations illegal.

"Garret was never an ordinary fourteen-year-old. He was tall, broad-shouldered, all that stuff and had a fake id. He would chuck down the strong stuff without breaking a sweat and fight with men twice his age. A confident young man who surely had a chip on his shoulder against the whole world and I was attracted to that."

Everything that Bill was saying seemed to be nothing new. Marg had seen it but somehow brushed it aside. The first time when she met him, she felt that he wasn't one to be easily intimidated but was one who was used to having their every demand met. Garret faced her brothers the night they saw him at the bridge with her, with a smile and didn't look fearful at all. Rather he told her that he would be okay.

"After your mom came to get me, the parents asked that whatever had happened, be kept quiet and Mr. Henderson warned me to stay away from his son. If I didn't, he would make sure that I paid for it. Garrett called and begged to meet with me the next day. He was on a rebellious streak, that's how he got the tattoo of a Phoenix rising from the ashes."

Marg pulled on a sad smile. The tattoo mystery answered, that her boyfriend had tensed up over.

"He was a badass in his day, right."

Bill laughed. "He very much was. We were at my apartment when the police busted through. I managed to escape and he didn't, having stalled them and once the police uncovered a stash of drugs, there was no way out for him."

Marg clutched at her throat at the news. Could Mr. Henderson have gone to that extent to make sure Bill stayed away.

Bill grasped her hand and stroked it. "How do you think he is able to relate with delinquent youths? I have heard about the things he has been doing. It's because of his stint in juvie. Mr. Henderson lil sis didn't plant anything. It was all on me and Garret took the fall. Six months that's all it took and the next time I met him, he told me to stay away. Look I shouldn't be telling you this. Garret is the one who should be clearing this whole misunderstanding because I am pretty sure that man loves you. All that I came here for is to apologize for ruining your relationship, especially after how good your mom was to me in clearing this whole mess."

Marg curiously looked at her brother. "Why now though? I get it that you want to apologize, but what makes you think he doesn't love you back. Maybe this person that I have come to know is nothing but a figment of my imagination and you know the real Garret?"

"I saw the way he looked at you the day you got engaged. That's what got to me the most. He was happy and not at all the person I once knew, who fought against everyone. That chip on his shoulder..." Bill shook his head and wryly smiled. "It was gone."

Marg slumped on the bench after Bill said that.

"Did—," she licked her lips that felt dry, knowing that Bill would not speak further about this. He very much preferred her to hear all this from Garret and besides Bill wouldn't know what happened afterwards.

"Did he ever say what made him be that way?"

Bill frowned.

"Please Bill, you knew him, in all this time I thought I did but I guess I don't even have a clue on the kind of person he is."

Bill sighed before he sat next to her and answered.

"Garret was molested from the age of six by his uncle. The family found out when he was nine and it was because Greg had witnessed it and mentioned it at the dinner table."

Marg burst out crying while Bill reached out and held her. Her heart ached for the little boy Garret once was and for Greg too, who at such a tender age had to witness that.

Is that the reason why he understood the grace of God so much to the point when he ministered, it rang true to whoever he spoke to? If Garret could be the way he was now, she looked at her brother after he dried her tears with a hanky. There was still hope for Bill.

"What about you?" Her brother laughed and tweaked her nose. He knew what she meant. "No sweetheart. I am beyond that. Garret might not have loved who he is and felt it was wrong, so yah, his faith changed him, but I am fine dear sister. I was never molested like him; I was born this way, from an early age, I had the inclination to guys like me."

Marg felt grieved then, but she merely hugged Bill and saw him off after.

Drifting back to the present, she slowly stood up from the floor, walked to the bathroom to wash her face, before she powdered it and left for the coffee shop. She had taken up a part time job too while she went to school. Her day as usual even though it was evening, was busy. A lot of people made the trip to the coffee shop because of the nippy cold weather.

She slowly walked back to her room afterwards. Tucking in her hands in the jacket to get the much-needed heat while her mind mulled over the impending nuptials.

How was she meant to proceed from here? Was she meant to make a call to him, congratulate him when she didn't feel that generous?

She lightly hit her aching chest with a fisted gloved hand, before she turned and walked into the road, her mind still not at ease.

One minute she was in the process of walking with a thought of reaching the other street, the next she was bodily accosted and her breath came out in a whoosh while a hooter blasted before the driver yelled at her, do you want to die.

Marg was failing to breathe, from the weight still on her.

"Are you stupid, you could have been hit. Didn't you see the light go red?"

"I can't—breathe," Marg motioned. Garret's eyes widened before he shifted away.

He gave her his hand. Marg huffed and stood up on her own, dusting her clothes while at it.

Why was her heart hammering like crazy and certainly not from the adrenaline rush of being shoved to the ground a while ago.

It had been three months but it appeared he still had the same effect he had on her before. Seriously, was she doomed to pine after him whilst he got married to someone else.

She looked up at him, braving the piercing gaze that would strip her of every wall and make her feel vulnerable and very much a fragile woman, like her father would describe her.

Still handsome as to be expected, nothing had changed. Guess he still kept an active lifestyle and didn't binge on food like she did, before she decided to hit the gym.

She might have thought she wasn't like her mother, but she did care about being in shape too.

Garret stared at her, just like he had been watching her across the street while she walked. Marg hadn't changed at all. What had he expected, that she would become haggard looking because she longed for him like he did her.

"By the way, I am not stupid." Marg said and glared at him. He nearly laughed, forever the defensive girl.

"Marg, can we talk?"

Marg reluctantly nodded and they walked to her hostel, each deep in their own thoughts before they came to her room.

She already knew that he was here to talk about his new relationship and its progress before she heard it from someone else, except for the fact that her mother had already informed her.

She placed her coat on the rack and motioned for him to do the same before she pointed to the couch and walked to her mini kitchen. "Cappuccino."

"Yes thanks," Garret answered in his deep voice.

This room held so many memories on how they first bonded.

They had both slumped on the bed, exhausted after trudging through every apartment in close proximity to the campus before she settled for this one.

The rooms were actually the best near the campus.

Reaching out to the Jacobs instant cappuccino in the box, she poured the contents into two mugs then the boiled water before she placed the teaspoons and walked to where he sat.

"How have you been Marg," Garret asked her.

"Fine and you."

"Good." A pause in which both of them searched for the right words, while they stirred their coffees.

"I..."

"I—."

They both laughed at having said it in unison.

"You go first," Marg motioned with her hand, while resisting the coldness that had suddenly sat in her tummy. Tightly clutching the hot mug, she watched Garret rub the bridge of his nose. How she had missed him doing that. That usually was an indicator that he was affected and not at all calm as he looked.

"Marg—I am sorry. I should have told you about my past from the onset."

"No, don't," she cut in. "I am the one who is sorry, for not hearing you out. Like you are aware, I am good at the judging area without giving anyone the benefit of doubt. I never thought that would be a painful thing for you to talk about. What your uncle did to you and how you coped with it after."

Garret grunted, "that's not it. How can it be when I don't feel the pain at the memory."

Marg was taken aback.

Garret took a sip of the coffee before he continued. "Marg when I was delivered it was like total healing to my whole being. I did have the memories, but they were not painful because when I did look back to that period in my life, I could easily see the hand of God and His grace over my situation. His redeeming power."

"Then why were you not able to freely talk about it?"

He softly chuckled.

"A beautiful tall girl who had once been my friend.

Her mouth fell open before she snapped it shut.

"You were in love!" she accusingly stated.

Garret chuckled at the angry glare. So like Marg to obsess over one fact without hearing him out.

"That's beside the point."

She cutely pouted her lips while he thought about how he had missed her.

"It was a year and a half after my deliverance when I decided to try dating. Ruby that was her name."

"Wait a minute you mean Ru-Ru the supermodel."

Garret nodded. Marg resisted the urge to flair her arms in dismay. Who in hell would compete with that? Knowing that Garret once loved her, didn't sit well in her heart.

When she had thought she would compete with a guy, as it turns out she now was meant to compete not only with Simone but also a drop-dead bombshell.

Maybe she should have paid more attention to her mom's lessons on how to satisfy a man, her mind hazarded while the other half thought her crazy in that she would contemplate to be like her mom.

Garret was frowning like he knew what she was thinking and wasn't happy about it in the least. She cringed at the morbid thoughts.

"Ru was my friend and it is now that I've come to realize that I didn't love her in the way one is meant to love a person they want to settle down with for the rest of their lives. We got on well together and I figured she was likely to understand me. When I told her, she didn't. Instead of hearing me out, she looked at me in disgust like she was seeing me for the first time. She didn't want anything to do with me afterwards"

Margaret's heart broke at hearing that. Hadn't she done the same? She was willing to believe the worst because of what she thought she had witnessed over the night of their engagement. All those months of knowing Garret and how good he was to her, flushed out in an instant by Bill's four damning words. I still love you.

Marg without realizing it had put her coffee mug aside and clutched at Garret hand in comfort.

"Despite having ministered to others of the hope found in the word of God, I realized that we had a long way to go in being accepted by people because of our pasts. Even to date people shy away when they learn that fact about a person. The men are quick to ostracize the person to the point, one goes back to the much more familiar ground than live as the new creature God describes in his word. Then, when Ru reacted the way she did, I was hurt and didn't understand why my past was meant to be the determining factor of my present."

Marg cringed. She was so much like Ru after all. Hadn't she tried to analyze his past actions, prob to judge and not to understand. When Garret didn't feel like talking about it, she had rather felt betrayed. She wanted to know his whole life while he insisted that, now is what mattered. "That was when I decided that it was too early to get into a relationship despite what others might have felt and so I left for the seminary." She drifted back to listen to what he was saying. "Four years down the line, I meet you Margie baby after a series of blind dates—," he corked his brow while she chuckled softly.

"You were very much different from Ru. Ru was reserved, mature I guess that's why I expected her to react in a much more mature manner than name shaming and all that, while you were a burst of energy, wore your heart on a sleeve for all the world to see. I knew you were attracted to me but didn't trust you to remain that way if I were to tell you. Ru, who had been my best friend, couldn't accept that history. What more you, an opinionated newly made friend.

A sob caught on her throat, as she thought of the day he commanded her to remove the pedestal she had erected for him when she heard him preaching.

Garret rubbed away the tear.

"I got further confused as I also happened to be attracted to you, and the lines of our little arrangement began to blur. Everything with you was new. I was the first man to kiss you, the first man to awaken your feelings so I feared to tarnish the image you had of me and of our relationship. Marg the Lord knows I tried to tell you, but my fear of losing you held me back. I had lost a friend already but with you I knew I was going to lose much more."

"I guess it's different with Simone then since you were able to tell her, and she accepted you," Marg added.

Garret looked at her in confusion, "Simone."

Her eyes widened. Had her mom lied to her, so she forced her into meeting Garret.

"Are you not involved with Simone and isn't it the reason why you are here? To inform me you are marrying her."

Who the bloody hell gave you that idea. Marg smothered a laugh. Yep this was definitely Garret, a work in progress.

Then she thought of what his mother said the day they got engaged. To think the same man had told her, he didn't do colorful language. She nearly snorted at the notion.

Then she thought of what his mother said the day they got engaged. To think the same man had told her, he didn't do colorful language. She nearly snorted at the notion.

"I came here for you Margaret. I wanted to see you, talk to you, reason with you if possible. I am a mess without you. I know it has taken me a long time to come, but I wanted to give you the breathing space, so you eventually accepted me as I am. History and all. My mom did mention you were now dating and the dude was about to propose too, which meant if I didn't come quickly, it would be too late.

Marg stifled a laugh. Their parents surely knew how to press the right buttons to make them move, seeing Garret was right there in her room and uttering the words he was meant to have voiced out to her three months before. They wouldn't have missed each other and been miserable the way they were, if only he had cleared the misunderstanding at the word go. Instead, he just had to be the proud rooster and she, the judgey one, hadn't realized it was his defense to not get hurt.

"Who is the guy by the way, who has taken my place?" Garret asked with irritation, lacing his voice. He was still possessive over her. This time Marg laughed loudly when it dawned on her that it has always been like that with him from the start. She was possessive over him to the point she ruined his date with Simone, while he made it clear that school better be what she wanted and not another man, since he was that man in her life.

Their little arrangement had been doomed from the start.

"Garret, there has never been anyone else, it has always been you," she finally said.

"Always me," he looked at her in wonder while Marg nervously removed her hand from his and stood up from the chair.

Garret stood up too and walked up to where she stood, near the window and reached out to her hand again. Her tummy fluttered.

"Marg, I know that I am the least likely person to ask this of you. You might foster fears that I will go back. I won't. This is proof of that." He directed her hand to his steadily beating heart

"What I feel for you Marg, I have never felt for anyone else. Besides, I'm too saved to remember what it once felt like to live in sin. The excessive drinking, the bad attitude, stick up my ass like I'm fighting against the whole world."

Marg giggled while Garret rubbed another tear that made it down her cheek.

"As for where my sexuality is concerned. Honey, I can't imagine being with a man when I have a lovely, beautiful woman like you, all soft, feminine and very responsive to the point she rocks my world and makes me horny like a teen. I am always battling, a hard-on whenever I am around you."

At that, Marg did laugh the louder and a few happy tears followed. This was the proposal she would have wanted to hear in the first place.

"Like I mentioned before, you are the only woman for me. I love you and only you. If you were looking forward to fighting with other women and men for my attention, I am sorry but you are a handful and more than enough for me."

She huffed as he echoed the sentiments she had entertained in her silly mind.

"Will you accept this imperfect man as yours Marg and for a lifetime."

Marg sniffled as she looked at the plea in his eyes. How she loved him, history and all.

Garret pulled her into his arms, and she was engulfed in the warm hug she has missed for the past months.

"Baby, please forgive me and let's start afresh, without any secrets between us. I promise I will never hold back and keep any secrets from you." He wiped off more tears from her face Marg smiled, cupped the handsome face before she leaned in for the kiss.

Epilogue

Garret and Margaret were married on the twenty third of December, two weeks after they had attended Cathy and Ralph's wedding. Marg had never looked so beautiful to Garret like she did then.

A few months after Garret and Margaret made up, before their huge fairytale wedding, Garret suggested a double date with her friends.

Marg knew why he recommended it, but was left stunned on how he handled the issue, once and for all. Margaret had felt that she couldn't stand by and watch her best friend destroy her life and hence broke the promise she made to Cathy to not tell anyone about her out of control relationship that had suddenly become over sexual and had her doubting herself.

To add salt to the wounded relationship, Cathy had a pregnancy scare that had Ralph all of a sudden being aloof and demanding on why she wasn't on family planning. When Marg heard that last bit, she nearly clawed out Ralph's eyes. He was such a typical man, who thought the decision to have sex and babies lay completely with the woman. With that unflattering picture of Catherine and Ralph's relationship, she told Garret everything.

Garret really could warm up a person to the point they got comfortable before he struck.

The day of their double date, Ralph was in a good mood and Cathy looked happy compared to the sad expressions she usually pulled on, when they were just the two of them.

Don't wreck the goods for someone else if you know you aren't buying."

Cathy choked on her food, hacked out a cough while Marg whacked her hard on her back. Ralph took a huge gulp of his drink and looked away from a serious looking junior pastor. Garret grinned and leaned forward on the table. "You see Marg here. The day we first got engaged, my gramps who we affectionately call paw-paw was out of the country visiting some relatives. The old man you should understand is a no-nonsense kind of person."

Marg giggled when Garret said that, since as it turned out, the grandfather had gone to extremes to make him wake up from his stupor. Both his gramps and father didn't dilly dally concerning the issues of life.

"One look at his future granddaughter in law, he gulped down the scotch he had been slowly sipping, winked at Marg and chuckled in glee. Already I knew that spelt trouble. Garret, he bellowed. Paw-paws bellow usually make my mom run for cover, you should understand that. He shook his head, goes like, "of all people, I never thought I would be forced to have the talk with you. The bees and the birds. Boy...he drawled out, what in the hell are you doing feeling the goods?" He married us off in an instant. Imagine that, the families were quickly called and assembled to witness before Marg and I made a mess of things."

His face turned into that of disbelief as he continued. "It's not like I had slept with Marg. We passionately kissed, petted heavily but never in any way tempered with that region." Cathy couldn't help as she had been trying to resist the urge to laugh out loud but as the pastor motioned over the table with his hands, she gave in. "The fact that I was playing around with the goodies was enough for my paw-paw. That white wedding, we professed to be waiting for, it was chucked out like it was nothing. Then he said after he married us in his loud bellow of course. Now you can touch and feel all you like."

Ralph threw back his head too and laughed at the hilarity of the situation. Apparently being consumed with one's passions wasn't alien, seeing the junior pastor couldn't resist his woman too. Garret and Marg must have been wallowing in shame, for them to be put on the spot like that in front of their families, he thought.

"You can go ahead and laugh. It wasn't a good feeling when the events were unfolding because Margie baby cried harder than I had seen her do. Her step moms surprisingly were quick to comfort her and tell her such was life. She didn't want to look at me and accused me of being on it, since I already knew how crazy my granddad could get. My family was the worst while hers was better, they did the virginity test and it ended there, they didn't fuss over a mere touch."

Margaret, Cathy and Ralph continued to chortle in glee.

"Marg is my wife," Garret said in a somber voice. "Now I touch her without that niggling feeling of it being wrong, it's okay. I am hers and she is mine. We aren't playing in the devil's field or arousing love before its time. That was what my paw-paw wanted us to realize. That there's a sense of security and overwhelming peace when you do the right thing. Since I consider the church my family and Marg still wants her big fairytale wedding, we decided to wait on consummating our marriage until the I do's are said in front of the church members. The youths can't wait for the feasting and dancing."

Marg smiled at Cathy, who was dabbing a few tears of joy from her cheeks.

"My point is," Garret stressed and looked at the couple. "Do right by each other. That's simple to understand, but the enemy makes it look like it's complicated while the stolen moments, the quickies that are easily accessible, for a while might be mistaken for the real thing. What stolen moments actually do, is to rob you of what's genuine and true, a good future and an extraordinary life you could have had, to a sad one that is full of negativity on what one thinks of the other. Sex was designed to be enjoyed in a marriage setting and never outside. Out there, it leaves you empty rather than fulfilled like it's meant to. It takes away, rather than give, two individuals getting as much as they can from each other, since they know eventually this madness will end. Instead of adoring and delighting over these precious bodies purchased with Jesus' very own blood, sex outside God's term is more of a selfish act rather than the unity brought about when two become one in flesh. Cathy and Ralph, God is gracious, He loves you and He wants you to experience sex on His terms. Whatever you have going on isn't worth it to lose the real gem only to have ashes. Christ never abused His bride and in the context of marriage, man is described as the head and Christ like. Ralph, if you love Cathy, do right by her. As a man that's what is expected of you. Don't shame her and make her into something she is not. Look at her." He winked at Cathy while she blushed profusely. "She is beautiful both on the inside and outside."

Ralph reached to Cathy's hand and squeezed it, smiling at her with all the love he felt while Marg squealed in delight. Now she knew why the ladies were crazy over Garett and would go to any extent to snag him.

He has always been an open book.

She thought of the days when she was getting used to him, while they pretended to be in a relationship, on how she had whined to her mother about him being busy all the time. If only she hadn't fought so hard in her attraction to him but had come into his world, all those questions she harbored would have been answered in an instant.

Garret was practical with the youths, real and didn't mince around. What people heard on a normal Sunday service, if he was the one preaching, was very much different from when he was one on one with the youths.

She could just as well imagine the Johnson sisters swooning and being revived in between his messages at how hard nails he could get. The youths were his life, including the prison visits he made, dragging her along with him. They worked to her advantage because she got the practical experience which she would never have gotten from just reading a textbook. Real people, with real issues. So, all in all, her imperfect man turned out to be perfect for her.

"Garret," his father called him when he was about to walk out of the house to the car. A few of the family members were now at the farm after the reception, including Beulah his mother-in-law who had come to see her daughter off.

She had been distraught since her daughter didn't shed a tear, while Marg had laughed and told her she knew she would always be a constant visitor at her new home so why cry?

Garret followed his father to the study and firmly shut the door behind him before he sat on the chair opposite him.

"Uhm here."

Garret's eyes widened when he saw what his father was handing to him. A box of assorted flavored condoms.

"In case you're not ready for the babies."

Garret stifled a groan. But it wasn't the end of it. He started receiving the talk on how he was meant to love Marg, take his time.

He abruptly stood up, embarrassed beyond measure.

"Son, I am not done."

"Dad we are; you are making me more nervous with your talk. I think I should have got this over with when I first married Margaret, rather than waited and built all these castles in the air that has you, my dear father, lecturing me on the basics," he said while his dad stood up and hit him on the back amidst his guffaws.

"And I thought I had it bad when I married your mom. Relax son, it's natural, don't worry."

Ya right.

"Is everything set?" his dad asked and he nodded before he walked to the door.

"Garret, aren't you forgetting something."

Garret groaned and took the box.

"Really!"

"Yes, really, unless you want Marg to be giving birth soon, then have to wave goodbye to that romance."

"Wait a minute, I thought you wanted those grandchildren."

His dad scoffed, "take your time son. Your ma started throwing up within a month of our marriage, by the time she reached her second trimester she didn't want to see my face. You should have heard the prayers I made then. I longed for the castles in the air more than the reality," He chuckled while Garret's mouth dropped open in surprise.

"Let's go," his dad said with a wink, "your wife must be tired of waiting for you." Garret walked out in a daze to the waiting car. Just like him, Marg had changed from her wedding gown, to a cute little dress that showed off her curves and tiny stature.

"Have fun on your honeymoon," all the family members present waved them off, while Beulah kept on sniffling on the side after she received a hug from her daughter.

Marg silently looked to her family as the car drove out of the farm.

"Do you think they will survive the night," Lucille asked while Graham scoffed. "With the way Garret was sweating rivulets of water, I don't think so. Just call your friend Martha to prepare the brew."

Lucille laughed and swatted her husband's arm while they got into the house

Marg groaned and sat back on the seat once she couldn't see her family and curiously eyed her husband. Mothers, that talk hadn't been palatable at all. Did they think she had grown under a rock, not to be aware of what she and Garret baby were about to do once they got to their destination. She shouldn't have mentioned to her mom that she and Garret had decided to wait even though having been pronounced as husband and wife a few months back.

Her mom was quick to point out that the anticipation and wait would make their night more pleasurable and memorable. They would tear each other's clothes before they made it to the room, really ma, did she have to hear all that stuff.

"And then," she motioned to the box, wide eyed and she could swear her man blushed.

"Augh."

Ok, so the hulk was speechless

"Give me that."

Garret chuckled at her expression and how she carried the box.

"Why are you holding it with the tip of your fingers like something nasty not meant for human consumption. It's a box, honey. A bloody box."

She rolled her eyes and joked, "a sweaty one love," and laughed when her husband looked at his hands.

"Did you drench your body in water, then put on your clothes after without toweling it."

She placed the box in her handbag before she squealed when her husband pulled her into his lap and said, "this sweaty mess is your husband."

She tried to scramble off from his lap but his hands were firm around her till she whispered breathlessly in defeat, "I give up."

That's when he loosened his hold on her but Marg didn't feel the need to sit next to him. Rather she cupped his handsome face and leaned in for the kiss she had been longing for throughout the day.

Not the chaste kiss they had shared in front of family, relatives and friends when they were pronounced by his grandfather that they were now husband and wife. Or the ones she used to receive, which would make her heart flutter, her toes curl and knees feel weak. His passion was always in check.

This time his movements were slow and deliberate, leaving a trail of blazing heat as he boldly stroked her arms and deepened the kiss, taking her breath away. She giggled as she tugged at the tie and removed it from his neck. This was her man, strong, confident in himself and very much in love with her, as evidenced by the deep probing stare that said it all. His love and respect that he had for her.

Thinking about how bold his voice had sounded as Garret recited his vows to cherish and love her for the rest of their lives in front of everyone, she knew that every word had come from deep in his heart and he meant it.

She was biased, since she still thought him perfect, her superhero from being Fletcher's daughter and Beulah's help. Garret shifted her legs so she straddled him before he pulled her neck and leaned in to continue with his passionate intoxicating kisses. One hand cupped her breast and a moan escaped her mouth as he continued to rub her nipple through the dress.

"You know dad was saying the female body is beautiful not aware I had seen my fair share of those including my delightful wife's."

Marg bit his lip and he yelped.

"Hey it's not my fault that you were always forward and looking for trouble. Tempting me like I was nothing but a stuffed teddy bear to you. Paw-paw was right in clipping those wings off."

Marg frowned and pouted her cute lips before she retorted, "Blame my parents damned genes."

Garret chuckled before he kissed those sweet, cute lips again. "I love you," he whispered after he drew away, to look and marvel at his wife.

"I love you more."

Who was she kidding, as much as her hormones had nearly made her lose her marbles, knowing Garret didn't take the bait but protected their love till the end, assured her that he was one person who strived in doing right by her, no matter how daunting that task may be.

She shivered at the warm hand that traveled on her thighs while her tongue ran on the seam of his full lips before she delved into the crevice of his sweetness.

A slight sound of the smoke screen opening was heard as the driver cleared his throat before announcing, "We are here."

Marg pulled away, coming back to mother earth. When she checked outside, she realized that indeed they had arrived at the airport.

A slight brush of her husband's hand on the nape of her neck had her quivering and inhaling sharply before she looked at Garret. He winked then looked at their bodies. Marg furiously blushed and scrambled off him.

When her legs were trembling like crazy and her whole body on fire, how could he still be so cool and unaffected.

"Marg shall we," he asked, having got out of the car. She grumbled and reached for his hand before she followed.

How could he be so calm? She furiously eyed him while she tried to refocus on her bearings and whispered, "Guess the talk went well." Garret silenced her with a hard kiss, that knocked off her sails, this time pulling her close and making her aware of his arousal before he said in a voice that almost sounded like a growl, "just because I don't reveal my emotions like a beacon, doesn't mean I am not affected. Would you Margaret Henderson prefer that I dragged you curve man style to my lair before I showed you what I really want to do to you."

Marg giggled, he really was a bad boy, considering he hid that side so well. And to think she had thought him to be innocent. As the saying goes, a man will always be a man.

Garret chuckled and on second thought, swept Marg off her feet while she yelped in embarrassment before he silenced her with a kiss. Marg moaned while her mind fought the embarrassment at the spectacle they were making as her husband strode into the cool building. She had unleashed the caveman.

Unknown to them, one of the fifteen-year-olds had called Martha and flawlessly pretended to be the father, requesting for the brew.

The brew that removed all inhibitions and made couples fulfill their every fantasies.

"Hey Dom," Greg called. Dom slid the phone in his pocket. He would return it to Mr. Henderson in the same manner he got it out of his pocket, without him being aware.

Congratulations Pastor Gee, hope you enjoy your wild night, he mumbled beneath his breath before he waved and rushed to Greg.

Marg giggled and enjoyed being in Garret's arms for a few seconds before he slid her back on solid ground, once they reached the check-in counter.

She couldn't wait to finally reach their destination and get to experience what they had been anticipating throughout, a fulfilling sex life which even the heavens smiled upon.

The End

If you enjoyed Garret and Margaret's story, I would appreciate it if you would help others enjoy this book, by recommending it to your friends and reviewing it.

BOOKS BY AUTHOR

<u>FAMILY MATTERS SERIES</u>

    1. The Inconvenient Marriage

    2. Finding a husband for Cissy

    3. A Risky Venture

<u>PERFECT GENTLEMEN SERIES</u>

    4. The Arrangement

    5. The Perfect Gentleman

    6. The Designer's Wicked Intentions

    7. The CEO's Hasty Proposal [Coming out soon]

<u>NEXT GENERATION SERIES</u>

    8. Sweet Crazy Love

    9. Loving a Compton

<u>ARRANGED MARRIAGE SERIES</u>

    10. The Pastor's Wife

    11. The Wrong Couple

<u>ROYALTY SERIES</u>

    12. The Prince's Bride

<u>INSPIRATIONAL ROMANCE</u>

    13. Amanda [Coming out soon]

    14. Leila

ABOUT THE
AUTHOR

Yvonne Sibanda loves a story with a happy ending. She believes that each and every one of us is affected by matters of the heart and therefore brings them out through her writing. To everything that has love in it, she is a softie, especially on emotional scenes of a movie or novel as she sheds a tear or two. Yvonne would like to hear from her readers, you can find her on the following sites:

Facebook https://www.facebook.com/vovosibbs

Once in a while, Yvonne drops a cover image of the latest book she would be working on. Information pertaining to promotions to her books can also be found on her Facebook page which you can use to your advantage by clicking on the links provided.

WordPress https://yvonnesbooks.wordpress.com

You can also read some of her work in progress at the above-mentioned site, including short stories she would have written for your enjoyment.

Yvonne is grateful for your support in her writing venture and thanks you all.

To God the Father, Son and the Holy Spirit, may your name be ever glorified. Amen

Synopsis

All that Margaret Fletcher wants, is to pursue her dream before she settles down. Her family has other ideas; hence she thwarts them at every turn.

Garret Henderson is tired of the disastrous blind dates he has gone through in order to find the elusive wife fit for a junior pastor. A disastrous date with Margaret Fletcher has him contemplating a little arrangement that might benefit the both of them. Unlike the other ladies he has met, Margaret has one ace above them, she is totally not interested in him.

Find out what happens when the lines between fake and real blur as Garret and Marg find themselves contemplating what they have been dreading all along. With crazy families and friends like theirs, what's to stop them from being further confused?